Even More TALES TO GIVE YOU Goosebumps

Look for more Goosebumps books
by R.L. Stine:
(see back of book for a complete listing)

#12 Be Careful What You Wish For . . .
#13 Piano Lessons Can Be Murder
#14 The Werewolf of Fever Swamp
#15 You Can't Scare Me!
#16 One Day at HorrorLand
#17 Why I'm Afraid of Bees
#18 Monster Blood II
#19 Deep Trouble
#20 The Scarecrow Walks at Midnight
#21 Go Eat Worms!
#22 Ghost Beach
#23 Return of the Mummy
#24 Phantom of the Auditorium
#25 Attack of the Mutant
#26 My Hairiest Adventure
#27 A Night in Terror Tower
#28 The Cuckoo Clock of Doom
#29 Monster Blood III
#30 It Came From Beneath the Sink!
#31 Night of the Living Dummy II
#32 The Barking Ghost
#33 The Horror at Camp Jellyjam
#34 Revenge of the Lawn Gnomes
#35 A Shocker on Shock Street
#36 The Haunted Mask II
#37 The Headless Ghost
#38 The Abominable Snowman of Pasadena
#39 How I Got My Shrunken Head
#40 Night of the Living Dummy III
#41 Bad Hare Day
#42 Egg Monsters from Mars

Even More Tales to Give You Goosebumps

TEN SPOOKY STORIES

R.L. STINE

AN
APPLE
PAPERBACK

SCHOLASTIC INC.
New York Toronto London Auckland Sydney

A PARACHUTE PRESS BOOK

ISBN 0-590-73909-3

12 11 10 9 8 7 6 5 4 3 2 6 7 8 9/9 0 1/0

Printed in the U.S.A. 40

First Scholastic printing, June 1996

CONTENTS

Even More TALES TO GIVE YOU Goosebumps

THE CHALK CLOSET

I wiped the sweat from my forehead. It was only seven-thirty in the morning. But the thermometer had already hit 95 degrees. And the air conditioner on the bus was broken.

This was not going to be a good day.

"Hey, kid," the bus driver yelled. "End of the line!"

End of the line was right, I thought. I jumped off the bus and checked out the school.

Millwood Junior High. It was a wreck.

The school stood four stories high. Its red brick — blackened with years and years of city soot — was chipped and crumbling. All the windows on the second floor were boarded over with plywood. And the roof sagged.

"Better get used to it, Travis," I told myself. I dragged myself up the steps. "You're going to be here all summer."

No matter what my mom says, I didn't exactly *try* to mess up sixth grade. Like lots of major disasters, it just happened. I tried to study. But stuff kept getting in the way.

Like when my cat, Lillie, had her kittens.

Or when my brother got a new computer game.

Or when something was on TV.

So . . . I messed up. And now, here I was in summer school. And looking at the school, I could see it was the pits.

I opened the rusty door and stepped inside. The main hallway was dark. I could barely see. The air was dry and smelled really stale. I started to cough.

I took a drink from the water fountain beside me. The water was warm and cloudy. And it tasted old.

I glanced up and down the hall. The place seemed deserted — no kids, no teachers.

No one.

I made my way down the hall and found a door marked PRINCIPAL. I jiggled the knob. Locked.

I checked out the classrooms. Empty. Except for the squeak of my sneakers, the place was totally dead.

What was going on? Was I here on the wrong day? Or was it the wrong school?

Then a voice broke the silence: "Travis Johnson?"

I nearly jumped out of my skin. I spun around and faced the tallest, palest man I'd ever seen.

"Y-yes?" I stammered.

"You're late, Travis," he said. His lips were unbelievably thin, and they hardly moved when he spoke.

Just great, I thought. My first day in summer school and I'm already in trouble. Way to go, Travis.

I followed the tall man to the classroom at the end of the hall. Of course, it was the only room I hadn't checked out. It was filled with kids. Many of them I'd never seen before.

Dooley Atwater and Janice Humphries were there. They came from my regular school. Janice was shy but okay. Dooley was the biggest goof in my whole school. He knew a million ways to get out of homework.

"The last row, Travis," the teacher said. "Be quick about it." Then he picked up a piece of chalk from the chalk tray and wrote MR. GRIMSLEY on the board.

Mr. Grimsley folded his arms across his chest and scanned the room. From the sour look on his face, I could tell he wasn't too thrilled about what he saw.

"Let me warn you, boys and girls," Mr. Grimsley announced. "I have very little patience with students who don't care to study. Got that, Dooley?"

"Me?" Dooley asked. "Why me?"

"I know about you, Dooley," Mr. Grimsley said, thumbing through a stack of cards. "I know about every single one of you. You're bright kids. But you're all lazy. Hear this warning. You won't get away with anything in my class."

Dooley smirked.

Mr. Grimsley glared at him. Then he continued, "You must do your homework every night — or be prepared to go to the chalk closet."

"The chalk closet?" one of the girls asked nervously. "What's that?"

"If you don't turn in your homework tomorrow morning, you'll find out, Amanda," Mr. Grimsley said.

"No teacher gives homework the first night!" Dooley protested. "You've got to be kidding!"

"I do not kid," Mr. Grimsley declared. "Now let's get down to work."

The first night for homework, we had to write five reasons we'd want to be a Pilgrim. As soon as I reached home, I sat down at the kitchen table and wrote down three:

1. Get to travel a lot.
2. Eat dinner with some really cool Indians.
3. Don't have to recycle.

Then my brother, Chris, came in. "Want to go to the Ice Cream Igloo?" he asked. "They have a new flavor — peanut butter marshmallow mint."

I didn't have a choice. I had to go — right?

After dinner there was a *Lethal Weapon* movie on TV. No way I could miss that.

So, when I arrived at school the next morning,

I still had only three reasons why someone would want to be a Pilgrim.

But it was three more reasons than Dooley had.

"Your homework, Dooley," Mr. Grimsley demanded.

"You have to give me a break," Dooley replied, "just this once, Mr. Grimsley."

"I have to?" Mr. Grimsley asked, arching his eyebrows.

"It kind of looks that way," Dooley began. "You see, a car alarm went off right outside my window. And it was so loud, I couldn't think. And by the time someone turned it off — "

"It was way past your bedtime?" Mr. Grimsley asked.

"Well, not exactly," Dooley admitted.

"But you did your homework anyway — and then when you woke up, the cat had eaten it. Is that what happened, Dooley?"

"Well, something like that," Dooley said, smiling a little.

"Sorry, Dooley. I don't give breaks," Mr. Grimsley declared. "It's time to go to the chalk closet." Then he stepped into the hall.

Dooley started to follow. But when he reached the doorway, he stopped. "I forgot my textbook," he said, turning back.

Mr. Grimsley grinned. A creepy grin. "The chalk closet isn't study hall, Dooley."

"So what is it?"

Mr. Grimsley didn't answer.

Dooley shrugged. Then he followed the teacher down the corridor. I heard their footsteps fade as they walked up the stairs to the second floor.

Mr. Grimsley returned in a couple of minutes — without Dooley. At recess, Dooley didn't show up. Or at lunch. Or the next day. Or any day after that.

I didn't miss him, and I didn't feel sorry for him either. I figured he was kicked out of school. And he had it coming to him.

But at the end of the week, the same thing happened to Marty Blank. Marty sat next to me. I didn't know him too well, but he seemed okay.

Grimsley handed back the homework he had graded the night before. I heard Marty groan when he received his. There was a big red *F* at the top.

"You didn't study, did you, Marty?" Mr. Grimsley asked.

Marty shook his head. "I couldn't," he said. "I had Little League."

"Little League was more important than your schoolwork?" Mr. Grimsley demanded coldly.

"It was the big game," Marty explained. "The team was counting on me."

"The chalk closet, Marty," Mr. Grimsley replied.

"But I did my homework, Mr. Grimsley," Marty

protested. "I'm not like Dooley. It's not like I didn't try!"

Mr. Grimsley picked up Marty's homework. "*F*," he stated. "I guess you didn't try hard enough — did you, Marty? Let me show you to the chalk closet."

Marty's mouth dropped open. It looked as if he were about to say something. But he didn't. He just followed Mr. Grimsley down the hall.

Four days later, Marty still hadn't shown up at school.

"Maybe Grimsley kicked him out of school," I told Janice. "Or maybe Marty convinced his parents to let him quit," I suggested. "For all we know, Marty could be having a great time at the lake."

"For all we know," Janice said, "Marty could still be in the chalk closet."

Janice and I gazed up at the second floor.

"That's probably where Mr. Grimsley took them," she said. "Those boarded-up windows give me the creeps."

We stared up at the windows in silence. "Travis, what do you think is in the chalk closet?"

"Chalk."

"Very funny, Travis. You might not be scared, but I am. I'm really scared. I got *D*'s on my last three assignments. What if I'm next?"

What if *I'm* next? I thought with a shiver.

* * *

The next morning, Janice's hands shook when Grimsley handed back our assignments.

"B-but I worked really hard on it," she stammered. "I really did."

I didn't need to see her grade. I knew from Janice's voice that she had failed.

Grimsley didn't say a word. He just walked to the door. And waited.

Janice stood up.

Grimsley waited.

She slowly made her way to the door. Then they both disappeared down the hall.

Mr. Grimsley returned in a minute or so, and the class went on as usual. Right before the bell rang, Mr. Grimsley made an announcement. "We're going to have a math test tomorrow. And I expect everyone to get an *A*."

An *A*? I'd never gotten an *A* on a math test — ever.

The bell rang and I dashed outside to wait for Janice. I thought about the test while I waited.

And waited. And waited.

Janice never showed up.

I ran all the way home and grabbed the phone. I dialed Janice's number. The phone rang and rang. No answer.

I looked up Marty's telephone number in the phone book and called him. A recorded message announced that the Blanks' number had been disconnected.

That night I tried to study. I never tried harder at anything in my whole life. But I was just too frightened to concentrate. What if Grimsley sends me to the chalk closet? I asked myself over and over again.

When I finished the test the next day, I knew I had blown it. I'd be lucky if I passed. But I'd have to wait till Monday — two whole days — to find out.

The weekend dragged. I couldn't think about anything except that stupid math test. And the chalk closet.

Monday morning finally arrived. My feet felt like lead as I walked up the steps to school. This was not going to be a good day.

I took my seat and stared straight ahead at Mr. Grimsley. He sat at his desk. The pile of test papers was neatly stacked in front of him.

He cleared his throat. "I'm going to return your test papers now," he said. "Most of you did very well."

He didn't look at me when he said that, I thought. But what did that mean? Was it good? Or bad? I didn't know.

"Bennett, Amanda," he began. "*A*."

Oh, no! He's calling out the grades, too!

"Drake, Josh — *A*. Evers, Brian — *A*. Franklin, Marnie — *A*."

Wow! I couldn't believe it. Everyone was getting *A*'s.

I broke out into a cold sweat. I wiped my sweaty palms on my pants. Hey, don't worry, I told myself. Everyone's getting *A*'s. I probably got one, too.

Grimsley continued calling out names and grades. I was next.

My temples pounded as I watched him stare down at my paper.

"Johnson, Travis — *D*."

The whole class gasped.

"You know, I — I can do better than that, Mr. Grimsley," I stuttered. "Let me take a makeup test. Okay? You'll see."

"No makeup tests in my class," the teacher replied sternly.

"Please, Mr. Grimsley!" I cried. "Don't take me to the chalk closet! Please!"

"Come, Travis," Mr. Grimsley said. "You don't want to upset the other students, do you?"

I glanced around the room at the other kids. A few of them stared at me. Their eyes filled with horror. But the others had their heads buried in their textbooks. They pretended that they didn't even know what was going on!

"Don't you care?" I screamed at them.

No one answered.

Mr. Grimsley stood at the door.

"Come, Travis."

My knees shook so hard I could barely walk.

I followed Mr. Grimsley into the hall.

The front door was at the end of the hall. Mr. Grimsley's legs were longer, but I was younger. Could I outrun him?

"Don't even think about it," he said, without turning back. "It's locked."

I followed Mr. Grimsley up the stairs. It was almost pitch-black on the second floor. The only light came from a naked bulb dangling from the ceiling.

I trailed behind Mr. Grimsley. Past Room 269. Then 270. Then 271.

When we came to 272, he stopped and turned toward me. "Good-bye, Travis," he said.

I took a step back. I couldn't speak. I was terrified.

Mr. Grimsley twisted the doorknob. Then he gave the door a little push. It creaked open.

I peeked in over his shoulder. My heart pounded. What would I see in there?

I couldn't see anything. It was totally dark.

Mr. Grimsley gripped my shoulder and shoved me forward.

I stumbled inside.

The door slammed shut behind me!

I was locked inside — inside the chalk closet!

I squinted. Waited for my eyes to adjust to the darkness.

And then I saw them.

Dooley. Marty. Janice.

And behind them, shadows of other kids I'd never seen before. Transparent figures. Ghosts.

I squinted harder. They were all doing something. They were all holding their hands up in the air.

Why? I wondered. Why are they doing that?

That's when I heard it.

That's when I knew the chalk closet was the worst place on earth to be.

My hands flew up in the air, too.

Up to my ears. To cover them.

To drown out the screeching.

The horrible screeching sound of chalk on a chalkboard — the sound that I'd have to listen to forever.

HOME SWEET HOME

"Sharon!" my little sister screamed. "Sha-RON!"

It always makes Alice nuts when I fool around with her dollhouse. That's why I keep doing it. I just can't resist.

It's bad enough to be twelve and still sharing a room with my little sister. But that dollhouse takes up way too much space.

Alice is always playing with it. She has a family of dolls that are the exact right size for the tiny furniture. They even have names — Shawna and Bill, the mom and dad dolls, and Timmy and Toni, the kids. They all have plastic hair.

"SHARON!"

I strolled down the hall to our room. Alice knelt in front of the dollhouse, putting everything back the way it had been.

"You called?" I asked.

She glared at me over her shoulder. "You changed the furniture all around again."

"So?"

"And you stuck Shawna upside down in the sink."

"Give me a break, Alice. Shawna is a doll. And in case you hadn't noticed, that's a fake sink. It's not like it's going to mess up her hair or anything."

"You are so mean!"

I made a face. "Get a life. Normal nine-year-olds don't spend all their time playing with stupid dollhouses."

"It isn't stupid!" she shouted.

"Is so!"

She stuck out her bottom lip and pouted. I felt bad. Well, a little, anyway. "Look, I'm sorry, okay?" I muttered.

I flopped down on my bed. Alice didn't say anything for a while. Then she set the roof back on the dollhouse and stood up.

"Sharon?"

"Yeah?"

"Want to ride over to a garage sale with me?"

"Don't you have any friends?" I asked.

"None of them can go. Besides, it's on East Bay Street, and none of us are allowed to go that far by ourselves. Please?" she begged.

I don't know why I agreed to go. I really don't. Maybe because I felt guilty for messing up her dollhouse. Whatever. A few minutes later, we hopped on our bikes and headed out.

* * *

We turned onto East Bay Street. Alice stopped in front of a big, old house set way back from the road. I spotted the name on the mailbox. "Hey, this is Mrs. Forster's place!" I cried.

"Uh-huh."

I glanced up at the house. A curtain twitched, and I had the feeling that somebody had peeked out at us. "Mrs. Forster is really strange," I told Alice. "At least, that's what I've heard. Some kids told me she has weird powers. They said she can change herself into animals."

"No way!" exclaimed Alice.

"I saw her one time," I insisted. "She's totally scary. She's got big, black eyes that glare right through you. Her hair is as black as her eyes, with a streak of white right down the middle that looks like a lightning bolt."

Alice stuck her tongue out at me. "What's the matter, Sharon? Scared?"

That got me. "Of course I'm not scared."

"So come on." She started pedaling up the long gravel driveway. I followed slowly. I didn't want to be there. Mrs. Forster *did* scare me. But no way was I going to look lame in front of my little sister.

Alice stopped in front of the garage. Two long tables had been set up to hold the stuff Mrs. Forster wanted to sell. But nobody else was there, not even to take the money.

"How come no one is around?" I asked.

Alice shrugged. "Maybe she's gone to lunch or something."

I turned to stare at the house. The windows seemed to stare back like black, rectangular eyes. "I guess we'd better go."

"Not yet." Alice pointed toward the nearest table. "There's a sign. It says 'Leave payment on the table.' "

"Too weird," I muttered.

"Well, I'm going to look," Alice replied. She dove in. I mean, this stuff was heaven for Alice. And I knew exactly what she was looking for.

"You don't really think Mrs. Forster is going to have dollhouse furniture, do you?" I teased.

"Even if she doesn't, maybe she's selling some lace or something I can use to make curtains. She's got some really old stuff here, and . . . hey!" Alice cried. "Look!"

She picked up a tiny object from the table and held it up. "It's a little doll lamp."

"Let's see." I ran my finger along the shade. It felt cool and grainy, like a frog's skin. A shiver went up my spine. "Yuck!" I exclaimed.

"It's perfect for my living room," Alice protested. "And she only wants two bucks for it — exactly what I brought."

She set the money on the table and tucked the lamp into her pocket. "Aren't you going to buy anything?"

No way. I didn't want anything that creepy woman owned. But I didn't want Alice to know how frightened I was. So I started poking through the pile of stuff on the far table. A big china bowl caught my eye. I thought it was kind of pretty, so I picked it up.

"Be careful with that," Alice warned.

A huge, hairy spider crawled over the rim of the bowl. It scuttled over my hand. I screamed and flung the bowl away from me. It shattered into a thousand pieces across the concrete.

"Sharon! Look what you did!" Alice gasped.

"I hate spiders!" I cried. "Hate them, hate them, hate them!"

I gazed up at the house. A woman stood at one of the upstairs windows, staring down at me. I could see the stripe of pale hair glinting in the sunlight. Mrs. Forster!

I panicked. I totally panicked. "Let's get out of here!" I cried.

We grabbed our bikes and rode like crazy down the drive. I glanced over my shoulder. Mrs. Forster remained at the window, glaring at me with her round, black eyes.

We didn't stop until we reached home. Alice ran upstairs with the lamp. I guess she forgot all about Mrs. Forster once she returned to her weird little dollhouse world.

But *I* didn't. That night, I dreamed about the old woman. In the dream, she knew me. She talked to me. “You broke my bowl,” she whispered in a harsh, raspy voice. “And you didn’t pay for it. But you will pay, Sharon. I promise. Now you are my problem. And I always take care of my problems.”

She leaned over me. Her hair fell down and tickled my face. I opened my eyes.

And found myself staring at the biggest, ugliest spider I’d ever seen. It dangled from the ceiling on a long white strand. As it swiveled to stare down at me, I saw a white stripe down its back.

It tickled my face with its hairy front legs.

“Mom!” I screamed. “Dad! Help!”

A few seconds later, Mom and Dad came running in. I scrambled out of the bed and flung myself at them.

“It’s a spider!” I shrieked. “A big, hairy spider right on my pillow!”

Mom clicked the light on. No spider. No spider anywhere in the room.

Only Alice, sitting up in her bed, her mouth open wide in surprise.

Dad checked under the covers and all around the bed. I kept watching for it to scuttle across the carpet.

But no. No sign of it. “It was right there,” I insisted. “It talked to me.”

Alice giggled. “Wow, are you messed up, Sharon. A talking spider?”

I forced a laugh, too. It *was* really silly — wasn't it?

The next day, I rode my bike over to a friend's house. I stayed longer than I had meant to. When I realized how late it was, I jumped on my bike and raced home.

By the time I reached our neighborhood, trees cast long shadows across the ground. One more block, and I'd be home. I checked for traffic, then started across the road.

"Huh?" I cried out as a car roared out of nowhere. I froze. Stared into bright headlights.

Then I swerved so hard my bike nearly flipped over. Tires squealed. I could feel a breeze as the car sped past me.

My legs started to shake, so I got off my bike and sat down on the curb. Wow! A close one! I couldn't understand where that car had come from. I'd looked both ways, after all.

A faint scrabbling sound floated up from the storm sewer beside me. I peered into the dark opening. I couldn't see anything at first.

Then something moved in the darkness. Something small and quick. My heart began to pound.

A big hairy spider clambered out of the sewer onto the curb. It had a pale stripe down its back.

I leaped up and ran down the block and into my house. It took me a while to get my breath back.

This didn't make any sense. Where were all the spiders coming from?

I didn't know the answer. But I did know one thing: I hadn't been dreaming last night. I kept picturing that pale stripe down the spider's back.

I shuddered. I suddenly felt so afraid. I didn't even go back out to get my bike.

After dinner, I headed upstairs to do my homework. Alice had dragged the dollhouse out into the middle of the room. Tiny chairs and tables, beds and bathtubs littered the floor.

"Hey," I protested. "You're trashing my side of the room. I can't even get to my desk to do my homework."

"So do it on your bed," Alice shot back.

I started to my bed — and heard a *crunch.*

"Oh!" I gazed down and saw that I had stepped on one of the dolls. Shawna. Her hand had broken off.

Alice instantly burst into tears. "Look what you did!" she wailed.

"It was an accident!" I cried. "I didn't mean to!"

"You did. You hate my dollhouse. And you hate Shawna. That's why you always stick her head in the sink. And that's why you stepped on her!" Sobbing, she grabbed the broken doll and ran out of the room.

With a sigh, I flopped down onto my bed. "Stupid dollhouse!"

I glanced up. My breath stopped. "No!"

The spider.

The spider with the white stripe.

It clung to the ceiling with its thick, hairy legs. If it let go, it would land on my face.

I shrieked and rolled off the bed.

When I glanced up, the spider was gone.

For the next couple of days, Alice wouldn't even talk to me. She walked past me as if I were invisible.

Just before dinner on Friday, I caught up with her in the hall. "Alice, listen," I pleaded. "I'm sorry about Shawna. I didn't mean to step on her. I really didn't."

She stared at me for a moment. "It's okay. Dad fixed her hand."

I felt better. But I just couldn't keep from teasing her. "I promise I won't put Shawna's head in the sink again," I offered.

"You won't?"

"Nope. I'll work on Bill for a change."

She stuck her tongue out at me. Then she spun around and headed for the dining room. Probably to tell.

I started after her. But then I heard the sound of glass tinkling above me, and gazed up at the chandelier. Its glass prisms quivered, sending rainbows shooting around the room. It happened every time a breeze blew in from the front window.

Except the window was closed.

The tinkling of glass grew louder. The prisms shook wildly. Before I could move out from under it, the chandelier broke away from the ceiling.

I dove to the wall.

The chandelier crashed to the floor beside me.

I shrieked and stared down at it.

Stared. Stared down at the spider.

"You — you tried to kill me!" I shouted at it. "I know who you are. I know what you're trying to do!"

I spun away. I had to get out of there. Away from the vicious old woman in her spider body.

I took three steps — and felt something drop heavily into my hair.

My eyes moved to the hall mirror. I saw it. I saw the spider in my hair.

I felt its hot breath on the back of my neck.

Felt its hairy legs slide through my hair, over my scalp.

"Noooooo!" With a cry of horror, I pulled at it with both hands. But it clung tightly to my hair. Clung so tight. So tight.

I screamed again. Couldn't anyone hear me?

I ran into my room. "Alice — help me! Help!"

She wasn't there.

And then I felt the spider legs — the points, the sharp points — digging into my scalp. Digging into my head.

Into my brain!

"Noooooooo!"

Over my scream, I heard dry laughter. "You are a *tiny* problem," the spider rasped. So close to my ear.

The pain shot through my head. Through my whole body.

"You are a tiny, tiny problem."

Was the spider growing bigger? I felt its hot, spongy body press against my back.

Was it bigger now? No. It wasn't bigger.

I was smaller.

I was shrinking. Shrinking fast. Standing in the shadow of the hideous spider that still clung to me. Still drilled its forearms into my scalp.

"I have my revenge," the old woman's spider voice rasped in my ear. "You are a tiny problem now."

"Noooo!" With another cry of horror, I broke free. Broke free and ran into the dollhouse. Hid inside the dollhouse.

I was as tiny as a doll. I could hide there. I could be safe.

My life now? It isn't as bad as it sounds.

Alice has fixed up the dollhouse really nice. I'm comfortable inside it. My room is really great. She even put in a little color TV!

I feel very safe and protected.

I just have one big problem.

Alice.

Here she comes now.

"Hey — put me down! I mean it, Alice! Put me down!"

Why does she think it's so funny to stick my head in the sink?

DON'T WAKE MUMMY

The day the deliverymen brought a mummy case to our house, I tried not to act scared. I knew my older sister, Kim, would tease me forever if she knew how I felt.

"Oooh! A coffin," Kim said. "Are you scared, Jeff?"

Kim thinks that just because she is thirteen and I'm only eleven that I'm some kind of scaredy-cat. She's always jumping out at me and trying to spook me. That's Kim's only hobby. Teasing me and telling me I'm a wimp.

Dad is the curator of the town museum. So I've seen a lot of mummy cases — at the museum. This was the first one delivered to our house.

It was all a big mistake. But Mom had the men carry it into the basement. She warned us not to go near it.

After the men left, Kim and I stood at the top of the stairs, looking down into the basement.

"I've heard about these mummies," Kim said,

narrowing her eyes. "They wake at night and search for prey."

"I don't believe you," I said.

"No, really," she insisted. "Mummies are jealous of living people. So they creep around after dark and steal the life from people."

"Well, that mummy isn't stealing anyone's life. That box is chained up tight."

"You know, Jeff, the worst thing about you is that you're such a wimp," Kim declared.

"I am not," I protested.

"If you're not a coward, then why don't you go down there and check out the mummy?" she demanded.

"No way!" I told her. "Are you crazy? You heard what Mom said."

"Why don't you go down there and touch the box? Touch it one time. I bet you're too scared to even do that," she said.

"Fine," I said. "I'll do it." I regretted it even before the words finished coming out of my mouth.

The light switch was broken in the basement. It was so dark down there, it even smelled dark, like clay. I walked down the stairs slowly.

The box sat in the middle of the room. Everything else was covered in a layer of dust. But that box was spotless. The lid was so glossy it seemed to glow.

Step by step, I drew closer to the coffin. The only sound I could hear was the beating of my heart.

The air felt cold and moist. I rubbed my chilly, sticky palms together, working up my courage.

You can do it, I told myself. There's nothing to be afraid of.

I reached out my hand to touch the shiny black box — and the lid moved!

The chains clanked.

My heartbeat stopped for a moment.

I couldn't help it — I screamed.

Then I turned and hurtled up the stairs without looking back.

The basement door was shut! Kim had closed it behind me!

I threw my body against it and burst into the kitchen.

Kim sat at the dinner table, laughing at me.

"The mummy is alive!" I shouted. "The chains rattled! The lid moved!"

She roared with laugher. "You're such a jerk."

She strode over to the basement door, threw it open, and peered down at the box. "There's nothing to see," she announced.

She was right. The lid was closed. The chains were in place.

My imagination had tricked me again.

Or had it?

*   *   *

I had a hard time getting to sleep that night. No matter how I twisted my body, I couldn't get comfortable.

Why couldn't I get to sleep? I looked around my room. Everything was in its place. My books stood up straight on the bookshelf. My computer sat on my desk, casting a shadow over a pile of notebooks. I had thrown my clothes on the floor and they were clumped together near the closet door.

Go to sleep, I told myself. Everything is fine.

But then I heard a *THUMP*.

I sat up in bed. It sounded like someone dropped the phone book on the floor.

I waited. I listened.

THUMP.

Again.

What could it be?

THUMP.

There was a rhythm to the sounds. One after another. . . . Sort of like . . .

FOOTSTEPS!

Each heavy sound was a footstep!

THUMP.

And the steps were coming closer.

Then I heard an eerie clanking. I strained to hear it better.

THUMP. *CLANK*.

My heart raced.

It was a chain.

THUMP. CLANK.

I gasped. The mummy! Searching for a victim. Searching for me.

I screamed, for the second time that day. I heard someone running.

My door swung open.

The mummy! It had long tangled robes and wild frizzy hair. I screamed again and dove under the covers.

"Shhhh," a soft voice said. "Honey, everything's fine. I'm here now."

"Huh?" Mom. Wearing her terry-cloth robe.

She sat down on the edge of the bed and rubbed my neck. "Did you have a nightmare?" she asked me.

"No!" I exclaimed. "The mummy is out. I heard it coming for me, coming up the stairs."

"You had a bad dream, that's all." Mom bent over and kissed me on the top of the head. She smelled like cinnamon and soap.

I listened to her footsteps padding off down the hall.

The soft sound her slippers made on the floor was nothing like the heavy steps I had heard before.

I wanted to believe her, but I knew what I had heard. The mummy was out. It would be coming for me again.

* * *

The next day, I biked to the library to try to find out how to protect myself from mummies. Would you believe that the only books they had on mummies were scary novels and art history books? Not one practical how-to book?

As I pushed my bike home through town I noticed a new shop on Main Street. The sign read SAM BONE'S MYSTICAL MERCHANDISE. In the window a tapestry was laid out, with all sorts of crystals spread on it.

Through the glass I could see a guy, sitting up on a counter, leafing through a big book. He had long, bushy hair and a beard. Maybe he could help me. No one else was taking me seriously. What did I have to lose?

I locked my bike up on a No Parking sign. Then I pushed open the door to Sam Bone's Mystical Merchandise. A tiny set of chimes hanging on the door rang out.

"Good afternoon, sir," the man said, hopping off the counter and closing his book. "How may I be of service?"

"Are you Sam Bone?" I asked him.

"The one and only," he said, doing a corny little bow.

"I'm looking for some information on mummies," I said hesitantly.

"Is this for some kind of school project?" he asked me. "Or are you planning a trip to Egypt perhaps?"

"No, you see, my dad is the curator at the Museum of Natural History here in town. We had a mummy delivered to our house by mistake. . . ." The whole story poured out of me.

When I finished, Sam Bone began pacing up and down the crowded aisles of the store. Every so often he would grab a book off the shelf and rip through it, searching for something. Or he would rummage through a box full of oils or candles or crystals.

"Of course!" he shouted suddenly. "I've got it!"

He disappeared into a back room for a moment. When he returned he was grinning from ear to ear.

He held a closed fist in front of my face and then opened his fingers one by one. In his palm lay a small purple sack, with pictures of gold eyes sewn all over it.

Sam opened the neck of the pouch and poured a tiny bit of blue powder into his hand.

"Mummy dust!" he exclaimed. "This is an ancient mix of minerals. It is said that the Egyptians would scatter this dust around the entrances to tombs to keep the spirits from crossing into the world of the living. One puff of this dust and a mummy loses its power."

Then he blew the dust right in my face. I coughed. The dust smelled bitter and old.

"I'll take it!" I shouted. "How much does it cost?"

Would you believe mummy dust costs twenty bucks?

"Aren't you scared to be in the kitchen, Jeff?" Kim teased me during dinner. "After all, the basement door is right there."

She gestured over her shoulder. "Doesn't it bother you that down in that box there's a dead body all wrapped up." She rose from her chair and started staggering around the kitchen like a mummy. "He's waiting for the night to fall so that he can sneak up to your room and — "

"Shut up!" I cried. What is her *problem*, anyway?

"That's enough!" Dad groaned. "Kim, you're not funny. Stop scaring Jeff."

While our parents were doing the dishes, I scooped out the ice cream. Kim leaned over the table and whispered, "If you think you're so cool, wait until tonight."

"What are you talking about?" I demanded.

"You know," she teased. "The mummy. I heard it last night, too, you know. And I also heard you screaming like a baby."

So I didn't imagine the sounds! Kim had heard them, too.

"I'm not worried," I replied. "I'm protected. I'm not scared at all."

"Yeah right," Kim said. "We'll see about that."

* * *

After everyone had gone to bed, I lay awake. It was chilly in my room. A storm picked up outside. The glass in the windows began to shudder as a sharp wind started up.

I clutched my pillow. Waiting. Waiting.

I gripped the pouch of mummy dust in my right hand. The feel of the small sack in my palm reassured me.

Rain drummed at the window. The room filled with white light. Thunder crashed outside.

Then I heard it.

THUMP.

From the room below me. From the kitchen.

The sound terrified me.

THUMP. CLANK.

I heard a low wailing moan. Was it the wind — or the mummy?

THUMP.

The mummy was coming for me.

But I wasn't going to wait for it.

I jumped from my bed and threw open my bedroom door. I couldn't stop shaking, but I made myself step out into the upstairs hall.

CRASH! Lightning lit up the hallway for a second. No mummy in sight.

THUMP. CLANK.

I grabbed the banister and jumped down the stairs, two at a time. My feet felt all prickly as they hit the polished wooden floor of the front hall.

I turned the corner toward the kitchen.

THUMP.

Something blocked my way.

The mummy!

Too scared to scream. My throat jammed up.

There it stood, in the shadows of the hall. The mummy hunched over, its face wrapped in strips of cloth. Its skinny arms hung limply at its sides. The arms were weighed down by hands that were huge — gnarled claws, wrapped in layers and layers of cloth.

The chains from the case were draped over its shoulders. They clanked as the mummy lurched up to me. Through the gauze over its head, I saw the mummy's evil grin.

Quick! I tore my eyes away from the ancient monster. I fumbled with the powder. Struggled to get the pouch open.

It was tied in a knot! My fingers shook too hard to open it.

The mummy moaned a low, ugly moan and reached its arms out to me. Huge, hideous claws. Reaching. Reaching.

Finally the knot gave way. I turned over the pouch to empty the dust into my palm.

Grunting, the mummy swung both arms at me.

I lifted my hands to guard my face.

The rotting cloth brushed against my skin. I stumbled back.

I hit the floor hard. My teeth clashed together.

The dust! I dropped it! The pouch fell to the floor, spilling the dust all over.

I scrambled to scratch up a handful.

The mummy growled. Lightning flashed. The ancient mummy flickered in the jagged, white light. Again I saw its evil, leering grin.

"WHO'S THERE?" boomed my mother's voice from the top of the stairs.

The mummy stepped away from me. The hall light flashed on.

To my shock, the mummy turned around and ran!

I couldn't believe it! Mom had saved me!

The mummy staggered to the basement door. It disappeared into the basement.

I slammed the door behind it. Then I grabbed a chair and tried to wedge it under the handle the way they do in the movies.

Mom rushed into the kitchen, tying the sash to her robe. Dad stumbled in behind her, fumbling with his glasses.

"What on earth is going on down here, Jeff?" she demanded.

"Mom, the mummy . . . it's alive. . . ." I gasped. "It was coming to get me, I swear! It's trapped in the basement right now."

"This has gone far enough," said my mother. "Larry, for once and for all, tell your son that mummies are dead and don't stumble around at night."

"Well, actually, there's something I didn't tell you," my Dad replied, rubbing his chin. "You see, there's a rumor that this mummy really is alive. I thought it was a joke."

"Huh?" Mom and I both cried.

Dad explained. "This mummy was given to us by another museum. They didn't want it anymore because the night guards said the mummy rose after dark to wander the halls. But the curator promised there would be no problem — as long as nobody took the chains off the box. The mummy can't come alive, unless someone takes the chains off."

"Jeff, did you take the chains off the box?" Mom demanded anxiously.

"No, no. I didn't!" I exclaimed. "Of course not!"

Dad jumped up as if stung by a hornet. "We've got to lock that thing in!" he cried. He searched the drawers till he found a heavy padlock. Then he locked the basement door with a loud snap.

"I'm so sorry," Dad said, hugging Mom. "I can't believe I put my family in danger. I never thought that the rumor might be true."

"I'm sorry I didn't believe you, Jeff," Mom said, turning to me. They tucked me in upstairs. With the mummy safely locked up, I quickly fell asleep.

Wow! It's really dark down here. Dad should fix the light.

I can hardly see my way down these stairs.

This basement is creepy.

I can't wait until Jeff and my folks go to bed so I can get out of here and go upstairs to sleep.

Oh, man! I almost got caught. But it was worth it — just to see the look on my brother's face when I reached out to grab him. He almost fainted, the little wimp.

Kim, you are so mean! But he asks for it! He really does.

Okay. Sounds as if they're gone. I'll sneak back upstairs. . . .

The door is stuck. Really hard. It won't open.

They must have locked it.

"Mom! Dad! Hello, can you hear me? It's me — Kim. I'm locked in the basement!"

No. The wind is too loud. The storm is making too much noise.

I can't believe this.

"DAD! MOM! JEFF! SOMEBODY!"

They can't hear me. This is awful.

I'm stuck down here for the night.

Well, I guess these old sheets will keep me warm. I can even wrap the gauze back around my face the way I had it before.

Of course this chain is completely useless.

Maybe it wasn't such a good idea to take the chain off the mummy case. But mummies have to have chains. Everybody knows that!

Good. Some lightning from outside. I can see where to sleep. Is that our old couch over there?

Whoa. Wait a minute! The lid to the coffin — it's off!

I didn't move the lid when I took the chains.

How did that happen?

Who opened the mummy case?

THUMP.

THUMP.

THUMP.

I'M TELLING!

It stood alone in the middle of the woods.

The most horrifying creature Adam had ever seen.

He crept toward it. Slowly. Silently. Through the bushes. Closer and closer to the hideous thing nestled in the clearing.

"I'm not afraid of you," Adam said under his breath. "I'm going to destroy you."

He ducked down in the tall grass and studied his enemy. He was only a few feet away from it now.

It was a gargoyle. And its huge, scaly wings rose over him. If the creature flew at him, he knew he could never outrun it.

I don't know if I'm brave or crazy, Adam thought. He crawled forward for a closer look. That's when he noticed the creature's claws. Long, sharp claws that could probably rip him in half.

"I'm not afraid of you," he whispered again. But

I am afraid of those fangs, he thought, peering nervously at the gargoyle's long, pointy teeth.

All the better to eat you with! Adam remembered the line from an old fairy tale.

Adam gazed up at the monster and took a deep breath. The creature sat silent and still. Good — it hasn't noticed me, he thought. Instead, it stared coldly at some twittering sparrows that had gathered at its feet.

It's now or never, Adam thought. He leaped to his feet and charged the monster.

"Eat this!" he screamed, lifting his weapon and squeezing the trigger.

Nothing happened.

The monster remained still.

Only the sparrows were surprised by his attack. They flew into the air with a soft flutter of wings.

"I don't believe it!" Adam cried. "I'm out of water!" He stared down at his empty water gun. Then he glanced back at the monster — a statue made of stone.

"You're lucky," Adam muttered. "If my gun was filled, you'd be dead now."

The monster didn't flinch. It was only a statue after all, stuck in the middle of a dried-up, old fountain.

Adam liked to come out to the woods and pretend to hunt. His best friend, Nick, said that pretending was for babies. "When you're in sixth grade, you've got to be cool," Nick told him. So

Adam came out to the woods by himself to play — when Nick wasn't around.

"If only I had more water . . ." Adam grumbled, shaking the water pistol.

To his surprise, the statue moved. Its mouth opened wide — and something green gushed out.

Adam jumped back.

Green liquid spurted from the statue's mouth.

Adam gaped at the gargoyle. "I don't believe this!" he cried. "It's amazing!"

Adam stared at the statue as the stream grew more powerful. The thick, green liquid splashed against the dry stones of the fountain.

"This is really weird," Adam said out loud. "Where is the stuff coming from?"

I guess I can refill my gun now, he thought. He pulled the plastic cap off one of the gun barrels and leaned into the fountain.

Then he stopped.

He felt as if the gargoyle were watching him.

He peered up at the monster. Its stone eyes remained frozen in a cold stare.

Get a grip, Adam, he told himself. It's only a statue. Nick would laugh his head off if he saw you now.

Adam reached up toward the gargoyle's mouth and held the plastic gun under the stream of liquid. His hand trembled as the gun's tank slowly filled.

"This stuff smells really gross! And it's kind

of gooey," he said, replacing the cap on the tank.

He turned to face the gargoyle. "Okay!" he yelled. "I've got you now."

Adam squeezed the trigger. Nothing happened.

He held the gun up to the light. He shook it some more. Maybe it's clogged, he thought. He turned and aimed at a large tree next to the fountain. He pumped the trigger, again and again. The gun suddenly jerked in his hands, and a green stream of liquid splashed the huge tree.

"Yessss!" Adam cheered.

The tree began to crackle.

Adam stared in shock as the brown branches faded to gray. The leaves crumbled. And fell heavily off the crackling tree.

A leaf dropped onto Adam's head.

"Ow!" he cried, rubbing his scalp.

The leaf was as hard as a rock.

Adam gaped at the tree. Was it true? Was it *possible*?

Yes. It had turned to stone!

Adam gazed down in amazement at the water gun in his hand. "Wh-what's going on?" he stuttered.

"I'm telling! I'm telling!"

Adam jumped at the sound of the high-pitched voice. A short, brown-haired girl with pigtails and freckles stepped out of the bushes. She pulled a red wagon behind her.

Adam groaned. It was Missy, his seven-year-old sister. The *second* most horrible creature in the world!

"What are you doing here, Missy?"

"Looking for *you*," she snapped. "Mom says you have to finish your art project. I told her she should take away your water gun. Or else you'll never finish it."

"You little brat," Adam muttered. "Why don't you mind your own business?"

"Why don't *you* do your schoolwork?" Missy shot back. "Do you want to stay in the sixth grade forever?"

"Go home, Missy," Adam said, fighting back the urge to tackle her.

"*I* always do *my* homework," Missy bragged. "*I* get straight *A*'s."

"Good for you," Adam growled. "Now leave me alone."

"What about your art project?" Missy demanded. "The contest is tonight."

Adam sighed. He gazed at the gargoyle in the fountain. Then at the stone tree. The crumbled leaves. He glared at his little sister.

"I'm busy," he said, clutching his water gun. "Art classes are for losers like you. I have more important things to do."

"I'm telling Mommy," Missy squealed. "You're in big trouble, Adam!" She stuck out her tongue. Then she started to sing. "I'm telling. I'm telling. I'm telling!"

Adam clamped his hands over his ears. "Shut up!" he yelled.

"I'm telling! I'm telling! I'm telling!" Missy sang louder.

Adam felt his face grow hot. Before he knew what he was doing, he raised the squirt gun and pointed it at Missy.

He didn't mean to squeeze the trigger. But he did.

Green slimy liquid squirted from the gun, splashing Missy's face.

Missy shrieked.

Then her small, round face turned chalky gray. Her lips froze in an open-mouthed scream. Adam stared in horror as the grayish-white color spread down her small arms and legs.

Then Missy's entire body stiffened. And a powdery dust swirled around her.

Adam's eyes bulged as he watched Missy turn to stone.

"Missy! No!" he shrieked. "What have I done?" he howled. "Don't worry, Missy. I'm going to hide you in the basement — until I can figure out what to do."

With a grunt, Adam hoisted his stone sister off the ground. She weighed a ton! He nearly broke his back lifting her into her wagon.

As he struggled to pull the wagon away, he heard gurgling. And hissing.

From the fountain? Yes.

Adam snapped his head around. Green slime dribbled down one of the gargoyle's fangs.

Adam shivered. His heart began to pound. He grabbed the wagon handle. Pulled as hard as he could. He didn't look back. He tugged the wagon until he reached the end of the woods.

All he had to do was pass by the school and turn the corner. His house stood on the corner of the next block.

He turned to Missy. "We're almost home," he said. "As if she can hear me!" he mumbled, rolling his eyes. He shook his head. My sister — a stone statue. How can this be happening?

Missy bounced heavily in the wagon. Adam glanced back nervously. He didn't know what would happen if she broke — and he didn't *want* to find out! He had to move fast. He didn't want anyone to see Missy like this.

"Adam! Adam!"

Adam recognized the voice. It belonged to the last person in the world he wanted to see. Mrs. Parker. His art teacher.

Mrs. Parker waved her arms in the air as she ran up the sidewalk after him. "Adam!" she cried out. "You finished your art project. I'm so proud of you!"

The tall, red-haired art teacher peered down at Missy's statue and clapped her hands together.

Adam gulped. "Well, Mrs. Parker . . . it's . . . not . . . um, really . . ."

"It's wonderful, Adam!" Mrs. Parker declared. "I had no idea you were such a talented sculptor. You've captured Missy in stone. It looks so much like her! It's a masterpiece!"

"But . . . but . . ." Adam fumbled for words.

"Hurry, Adam! Take your sculpture into the school. The art contest has already begun. Maybe you'll win first prize!"

Adam sighed. He stared at his stone sister. He wondered if she could hear. He wondered if she could *think*.

"Sorry about this, Missy," he whispered. "Nothing I can do now." He pulled the wagon into the school.

Adam won first prize. The judges placed a blue ribbon on Missy's stone shoulder. Mrs. Parker congratulated him.

His friend Nick came up and slapped him on the back. "Cool project," he said. "Really cool. It looks just like your bratty little sister! Want to come over and play video games?"

"Um. I can't," Adam stammered. "I — uh — have to get home and baby-sit Missy."

"Okay, see you," Nick said. He took one more look at Adam's statue. "Really amazing. How did you do that?"

Adam brought the wagon into the auditorium.

He crouched down to lift Missy up. And almost dropped her when he heard the voice. Missy's voice.

"Help . . . me . . . Adam."

Adam gasped.

"Did you say something, Adam?" Mrs. Parker asked.

"No," Adam replied. He grabbed the wagon handle, tugged hard, and raced out of the school.

Adam started toward his house when he spotted his parents in the front yard. Admiring their vegetable garden.

"Oh, no!" he moaned. "We can't go back to the house," he told Missy. "Not yet."

He didn't know where to go. So he hauled Missy back into the woods. "We'll hide near the fountain until I can sneak you into the house," he told her.

The sky was darkening as evening approached. The wind howled through the trees. A shiver ran down Adam's spine.

He pulled the wagon into the clearing.

And screamed. "Nooooooo!"

The gargoyle was gone.

"Where is it?" Adam cried. "Where — ?"

Adam didn't finish. A shadow slid over him. He glanced up in time to see the huge wings.

The gargoyle was flying!

No time to duck. No time to run.

In a gust of sour air, the ugly creature swooped

down. Its heavy wings pounded Adam's head.

"Get away from me!" he shrieked, throwing his arms up. "Get away!"

The giant creature swooped down again. Its eyes glowed a deadly red. Adam couldn't get away. The gargoyle dug its sharp claws into his shirt, shredding the sleeve.

"Noooo!" Adam uttered a terrified wail.

The gargoyle soared up again and began to circle. Prepared to dive again, its eyes flaming angrily.

Green ooze seeped from its gaping mouth. The liquid hit Adam's cheek with a sickening splat. His face sizzled.

Adam wiped the ooze away. He felt dizzy. Faint.

The gargoyle soared down at him. Adam dodged the monster.

As the gargoyle plunged toward him again, Adam spotted the water gun on the ground.

"Yes!" He grabbed it. Waited for the creature to swoop in closer . . . closer . . . closer.

When he could feel its sour, cold breath on his face, Adam pulled the trigger.

A blast of the slimy liquid splashed over the monster's glowing eyes.

The creature opened its mouth in a hideous howl. Then it dropped to the ground with a heavy thud.

And became a stone statue again.

Green liquid trickled from its leering mouth and dripped down its fangs.

"Yes!" Adam cried happily. "I did it! I did it!"

"Help . . . me . . . Adam."

"Missy!" Adam had forgotten all about her.

What am I going to do? he asked himself in a panic.

An idea flashed into his terrified thoughts. He reached for his water gun. It had some green liquid in the tank.

Adam shrugged. It was worth a try.

He aimed at the Missy statue. He held his breath and squeezed the trigger.

Nothing happened at first. Then, slowly, the gray stone cracked and crumbled. Layers of dust flaked from Missy's face. Her arms. Her legs.

"Adam, you jerk!" her voice rang out angrily from the rubble. "How could you do that to me?"

Adam grinned and hugged Missy. "You're alive!" he cried. He happily brushed the dust off her clothes.

"No thanks to you, stupid!" she snapped.

Adam ignored her angry words. He was so happy to see her. So happy! He threw his arm around her shoulders and led her through the woods.

"I can't believe you put me in the art contest," she complained, shoving his arm away. "They put that stupid blue ribbon on me. I felt like a total jerk!"

Adam sighed.

"Wait until I tell Mom. You'll be in big trouble! I'm telling her everything. I'm telling! I'm telling!"

Adam stopped walking. "Please, Missy — " he started.

"I'm telling! I'm telling! I'm telling!" she chanted nastily.

Adam sighed again. "I don't think so," he said softly.

Then he aimed the water pistol at her and pulled the trigger.

THE HAUNTED HOUSE GAME

I opened the closet door and reached up to the top shelf. It was dark up there. I couldn't really see anything, so I groped around until my fingers found what I was searching for.

"Aha. Here it is!" I said, carrying the box over to the table. "We're going to play Haunted House."

"Oh, Jonathan," Nadine moaned. "Not that dumb game again!"

"Come on," I replied, opening up the box. "It's fun. It's really scary."

"Yeah, that game is dumb," Noah echoed.

"Can't we play Parcheesi?" Annie complained.

"This is better," I said. "There aren't any ghosts in Parcheesi."

"But we've played it a hundred times before," Nadine mumbled.

"It's always different," I insisted. "Come on. Let's play Haunted House."

I unfolded the game board and lined up the

playing pieces. *BOOM!* A booming thunderclap shook the house.

We all turned to stare out the big picture window. The rain beat against it — hard. A bolt of lightning sliced through the sky. Then — *BOOM!* More thunder.

There are three things I really hate. The first one is thunder. The second — lightning. And the third — baby-sitting my seven-year-old brother and sister, Noah and Annie. Tonight I was a three-time loser.

At least Nadine is here, I thought. I stared at her across our long, oak dining-room table. Nadine is my best friend. We're in the same sixth-grade class. Whenever our parents go out together, Nadine gets to sleep over.

I dropped the dice in the little cup that came with the game. As I swirled them around, another burst of thunder startled us.

The house rumbled. Every window shook. And we have a lot of windows. Thirty-nine to be exact. I know. Because I counted them the last time I baby-sat the twins — when we played the Let's Count the Windows game.

"I wish Mom and Dad would get home," I said as I swirled the dice some more.

"Jonathan is afraid of thunder," Annie chirped.

"And lightning." Noah grinned.

"I am not," I protested, feeling my face turn hot. "Let's start," I said.

"What are the rules again?" Noah asked.

"The object of the game," I explained, "is to go around the board, through the haunted house — and try to find the hidden ghost."

"Oh, yeah. Now I remember," Noah said.

"And don't forget," I said in my best scary voice. "Be very careful. Don't land on SCARED TO DEATH!"

I shook the dice up and down in the little cup. Then from side to side. Then up and down again.

"Come on, Jonathan," Nadine said. "Roll the dice."

I tilted the cup and the dice spilled out. "Seven," I announced. "Lucky seven!"

"One-two-three-four-five-six-seven," I counted. I moved my green marker seven spaces.

And landed on YOU HEAR CREAKING FOOTSTEPS ON THE STAIRS.

I placed my marker down on the square.

Creeeak.

"Did you hear that?" I whispered.

Nadine and the twins nodded.

Creaking footsteps on the stairs. The stairs that led to our bedrooms.

"Maybe it's the cat," Annie whispered.

"Yeah, maybe it's the cat," Noah echoed.

"We don't have a cat," I replied.

We sat hunched around the table. Listening. Everything remained quiet. Everything except my heart pounding in my chest.

"Hey! I know what it was," Nadine said, straightening in her chair. "I bet the hall window is open upstairs. It was just the wind blowing through the window."

"That's it," I said, not totally convinced. It definitely sounded like a creak to me.

I studied everyone's faces around the table. No one appeared worried. "Okay, Annie. It's your turn. Spin," I said.

"You don't spin, Jonathan. You roll," Annie declared.

"Go ahead, Annie," Noah whined. "Take your turn."

"All right," Annie replied. She slowly tilted the cup and the dice dribbled out. "Three!"

Annie moved her red marker three spaces. "Onnnne. Twoooo. Threeee."

And landed on WIND RATTLES THE WINDOWS.

She placed her marker on the square and — the wind outside started howling. Really loud.

Then all the windows in the house began to rattle. All thirty-nine of them. First with a tinkling sound. Then more forceful. Vibrating in their frames.

The gusts outside grew stronger. Meaner. They whipped the windowpanes. I thought the glass would shatter.

My hands began to tremble. I hid them under the table.

I glanced over at Nadine. She stared out the big picture window.

I shifted my gaze to the twins.

The twins!

They were gone!

"Annie! Noah!" I cried.

"Here." Two small voices called from under the table.

"Come on out," I urged. "Everything's okay." But I wasn't as sure about that as I sounded.

"I'm staying here," Annie answered. "This game is too creepy. Every time we land on something, it really happens."

"It's not the game," I said. "It's the wind. And it's not blowing anymore."

It was true. The howling had quieted to a soft whistle. The windows stopped rattling.

"Jonathan is right," Nadine backed me up. Then she peeked under the table. "It's your turn, Noah. Don't you want your turn?"

"Of course I want my turn," he replied. He popped up and landed in his chair. He tossed the dice into the cup.

Annie slowly surfaced and plopped into her seat. "Let's play fast," she begged.

Noah swirled the dice and rolled a 2. He pounded the board with his blue marker.

My eyes darted to the board to see where he would land.

I found the square.

Noah plopped his marker down on it.

It said YOU HEAR AN EERIE MOAN.

A quick bolt of lightning pierced the sky. And then we heard it.

A moan.

A low, sad moan. From somewhere — inside the house.

"There's a ghost in here!" Annie shrieked. "Hide!"

"Where?" I yelled.

"In the closet!" Annie cried, jumping up from her chair.

"How do you know it's in the closet?" I shouted.

"She means we should *hide* in the closet," Nadine said. "Will everyone please stop screaming."

We stopped. The room fell silent. No creaking. No rattling. No moaning.

"There's no one here but us," Nadine continued. "This house always makes weird noises when it rains."

I guessed Nadine was right. She seemed so sure of herself. But I didn't think the problem was house noises.

"Now," Nadine said, scooping up the dice. "It's my turn."

She rolled a 4. I watched her closely. I was afraid — afraid to see where she would land.

Nadine moved her marker four spaces. And plunked it down on THE LIGHTS GO OUT.

And we all screamed as the lights went out.

"Everybody, sit still!" I shrieked. "I'll find some candles."

I groped my way into the kitchen. Mom and Dad kept candles in here somewhere. But where?

I couldn't see my own hands in front of my face. How was I supposed to find those candles? I opened every drawer in the kitchen, fumbling for them.

"Can you hurry up?" Nadine called from the dining room.

"Sure, Nadine," I muttered. "No problem."

Aha! Found them! Right on the counter. In their holders. Where they always are. I lighted them and returned to the other room.

We gathered at the end of the table — around the candles. Annie and Noah's eyes flickered with fear.

I was afraid, too.

"I don't want to play this game anymore," Annie whimpered. "It's too scary!"

"Our house is haunted." Noah's voice quivered.

"It's not the house," Annie whispered. "It's the game. This game is haunted."

I grabbed the dice and jiggled them in the cup. I glanced around the table. Everyone's eyes were opened wide. Glued to the board.

Lightning flashed outside the window. The candles sputtered in the dark.

Should I roll the dice? I wondered, gazing at our shadows dancing on the walls.

Should we stop playing?

Get serious, Jonathan, I told myself. It's only a game.

I spilled out the dice. 5.

I moved my marker. Slowly.

I held my breath as it landed on YOU HEAR A SCREAM IN THE ATTIC.

We sat quietly. Listening.

And then we heard it.

From upstairs.

A terrifying scream!

"Wh-what was that?" I stammered.

"Uh. The storm," Nadine replied. "Just the storm. Your turn, Annie."

I knew Annie didn't want to play anymore. But she rolled the dice. And moved her marker six spaces.

"YOU HEAR A BONY HAND TAPPING ON THE WINDOW." I read the words in the space.

No one spoke.

The room remained silent.

No tapping.

"See?" I said, walking over to the window. "Everything's — "

BANG!

A hand! A pale, bony hand — flew up out of nowhere! It banged the window hard.

The twins shrieked. I leaped back.

The wind picked up, and an icy draft blew through the dining room. The candles flared.

Nadine wrapped her arms around herself. Annie shrank back in her chair.

I studied the game board. Then I wiped my clammy hands on my jeans as Noah picked up the dice. *Not a three! Not a three!* I chanted to myself as Noah prepared to throw.

The dice tumbled out of the cup. They rolled. And rolled.

And stopped on — 3!

SCARED TO DEATH!

A candle blew out. Blinding white lightning flashed through the room. We screamed. And screamed. It seemed as if we screamed for hours.

The windows shuddered and quaked. Footsteps creaked on the stairs. An eerie moan floated up from the basement and flooded the room.

And then we heard the terrifying tapping.

Tapping. Tapping. Tapping.

We couldn't see it in the dark. But we knew what it was. The bony hand. Tapping against the window.

And then we were screaming again. Screaming so loud, it drowned everything out. Screaming so hard the whole house seemed to disappear.

I screamed until I couldn't hear myself.

Screamed until I couldn't breathe.

And then I stopped screaming, and the silence felt good.

I ran to the front door. I had to get out of that house. I had to!

But I stopped to pick up the newspaper on the mat. A yellowed newspaper.

The candle glow washed over the bold headline:

4 KIDS DIE IN MYSTERY DEATH!

My eyes rolled over the first paragraph:

> Police were completely baffled when they found four kids dead in an old mansion last night. "It looked to me as if they were scared to death!" declared one police officer.

Scared to death. Scared to death.

I glanced at the date on the newspaper. March 14, 1942.

So *that's* when we died, I realized. We died over fifty years ago. And we've been haunting this old house ever since.

I couldn't stay at the door. Nadine and the twins were waiting at the table for me.

Rain beat hard against the windows. The lights flashed back on. I opened the closet door and reached up to the top shelf. It was dark up there. I couldn't really see anything, so I groped around until my fingers found what I was searching for.

"Aha. Here it is!" I said, carrying the box over to the table. "We're going to play Haunted House."

"Oh, Jonathan," Nadine moaned. "Not that dumb game again!"

"Come on," I replied, opening up the box. "It's fun. It's really scary."

"Yeah, that game is dumb," Noah echoed.

"Can't we play Parcheesi?" Annie complained.

"This is better," I said. "There aren't any ghosts in Parcheesi."

"But we've played it a hundred times before," Nadine mumbled.

"It's always different," I insisted. "Come on. Let's play Haunted House."

CHANGE FOR THE STRANGE

Jane Meyers, twelve-year-old track star. That's me. As I stepped up to the starting line, I could hear the crowd scream. The fans roared. They were waiting. Waiting to see my spectacular long jump.

"Jane? Jane? Earth to Jane."

"Huh?"

"Jane — stop daydreaming. It's time to go!" Lizzy called from across the practice field.

Lizzy Gardner is my best friend. I watched as she walked toward me, careful to keep away from the dirt patches. Lizzy hates to get her shoes dirty. Today she wore sparkly pink sneakers and a short pink skirt. A pink headband held her blond hair in place.

"Are you ready to go?" she yelled, cupping her hands around her mouth.

Lizzy doesn't understand anything about track or why I practice so much. She thinks I'd have more fun at her house, hanging out.

But I want to be a track star more than anything else. Unfortunately, I didn't make the school team. I heard one of the girls on the team say I wasn't good enough to carry their towels.

That was so cold. But I'm not giving up. Every afternoon after school, I practice out in the field. Some day I'm going to be an incredible jumper. No matter what it takes.

After I practice, I always hang out at Lizzy's house. First we watch *Animaniacs*. Then we put on the CD player and dance around to our favorite band, Fruit Bag.

Sure, it's fun. But lately I've been more into track than hanging out.

Lizzy has changed, too. She still wants me to come over and do the same things — only now she's added a new one. She likes to go through her closet, thinking up new outfits.

"Do these shoes go with my new skirt? Does this top match my eyes?"

We do that until Ivan the Terrible barges into her room. That's what we call Lizzy's little brother. Ivan has a dog. A really mean pit bull. He named it Lizzy — just to make his sister angry.

Lizzy the dog ate Lizzy the person's new yellow scrunchy last week. He swallowed it in one gulp.

Ivan also has a whole collection of mice, snakes, and other weird animals. He likes to chase us all over the house, dangling his disgusting creatures in our faces.

"Hello! Anybody home?" Lizzy tapped me on the shoulder. "I've been talking for five minutes. And you haven't heard a word I've said."

By now, I'd gathered my things together. "Sorry," I said as we headed off the practice field. "What's up?"

"Before we go to my house," Lizzy told me, "I want to go shopping. I found a great clothing store. It's called A Change for the Strange. Have you seen it? It's right around the corner."

I shook my head no.

A minute later, we stood in front of the store. A neon pink-and-orange awning stretched over its front door. A CHANGE FOR THE STRANGE ran across the top in glowing letters.

I walked through the door and gasped.

The place was so . . . strange. It didn't seem like a clothing store at all. All sorts of weird items crammed the aisles.

Rain slickers hung from moose antlers. Yellow umbrellas with duck-head handles bobbed in puddles of water.

Green capes with velvet flowers dangled from leafy trees. Fluffy bunny slippers peeked out of rabbit hutches. Shark's-tooth necklaces floated in a tiny wave pool.

Lizzy disappeared between the racks. I usually

follow her around stores like a little kid. But this time, I stood in one place, gawking.

A store clerk stepped up to me. "May I help you?" she asked.

Something *had* caught my eye — a bright red jacket. It had tiny cracks in the material and a yellow trim that ran around the middle.

"Can I see that jacket?" I asked.

The clerk reached up and unhooked the jacket from a tree branch. The jacket looked wet. Slick. But when I ran my hand down the front, it felt totally dry.

"It's a cool-looking pattern," I told her.

She smiled and pointed to the cracks. "Those are scales," she explained. "That jacket is snake-skin."

"Ugh!" I snatched my hand away.

The salesclerk slipped the jacket off the hanger. "Try it on," she urged. "I bet it will look great on you."

I slipped into it, then I turned toward the mirror. It looked great. I twirled around. A perfect fit!

"I'll take it!" I declared.

"You will?" Lizzy came over, surprised.

"Sure. It looks great with my eyes!" I joked.

Lizzy grinned. "I told you this store was great." She held out a pair of white bunny slippers. "I'm going to buy these."

I choked back a giggle. A snakeskin jacket was one thing. But bunny slippers? "Those will be great for when you get hopping mad!" I teased Lizzy.

"Ha-ha. Remind me to laugh later," Lizzy snapped.

We quickly paid for the clothes and rushed out of the store.

Out on the street, I zipped up the snakeskin jacket all the way to my neck. I hadn't taken it off since I tried it on — not for a second. I loved it!

I gazed at the bright snakeskin as we walked. It sparkled in the sunlight. It looked awesome — like something a model would wear.

When we reached Lizzy's house, we spotted Ivan crawling around the front yard. "Shh!" he whispered. "I'm on the lookout for caterpillars. I'm starting a new collection. So don't scare them away."

"No problem!" Lizzy shouted as loud as she could. Then she stamped her feet and waved her arms. "We'll be so quiet, you won't even know we're here!" she screamed.

I started to follow Lizzy into the house, then stopped. I felt kind of weird. Kind of weak. And dizzy.

"Are you okay?" Lizzy asked. "You look a little pale."

"I'm not sure," I answered. I took a few more

steps. Everything around me started to spin. I grabbed onto Lizzy so that I wouldn't fall.

"Maybe you're getting sick," Lizzy said. "Want me to walk you home?"

"No, that's okay," I replied weakly. "I can go by myself."

"Are you sure? You don't look good."

"I'll be fine," I told Lizzy. "I'll call you when I get home."

I started home, but I didn't get very far.

Suddenly I felt really hot. My skin felt as if it were burning up.

All I wanted to do was lie down, right there on Lizzy's lawn. Stretch out in the cool green grass.

But I forced myself to stand.

Then I flicked out my tongue.

It darted in and out. In and out.

I tried to stop. To hold it in. But I couldn't!

And each time it lashed out, it grew longer. Pointier.

I clamped my mouth shut. But my tongue shot back out. And I smelled something strange.

An animal.

A cat. Then I smelled a dog and a squirrel.

My mind raced with panic. I could never smell animals before. What was happening to me?

Then I sniffed something really tasty. A nice mousy smell coming from Lizzy's house. Ivan's pet mice! Mmm-mmm!

I clutched my head.

And then I screamed. "My head!"

I had no hair! No ears! My whole head was covered with dry, cracked skin.

I rubbed it frantically. I wanted to bring back my old head.

Then the world seemed to tilt. Everything swam out of focus, as if I were on a speeding merry-go-round. I couldn't hold myself up. I sank to the ground.

I closed my eyes. "I'll count to three," I said. "Then everything will be okay. I'll wake up and be back to normal."

Slowly I counted — one, two, three. I opened my eyes.

And I shrieked out in terror.

I wasn't Jane Meyers, track star. I wasn't even Jane Meyers, human being.

"I'm a snake!" I tried to shout. But a long *hisssss* was all that came out.

I felt sick to my stomach. I was a snake! A slithering, fork-tongued snake!

I need help, I thought desperately. I need Lizzy! She'll know what to do. I nosed aside a giant blade of grass and stared up at Lizzy's house.

How could I get inside?

I started to slither toward her front door — when her mother opened it! She stood in the open doorway, fumbling for something inside her bag.

This was it — my chance to get inside!

I slithered as fast as I could. Then a shadow fell over me.

Lizzy — the pit bull.

"Oh, no!" I tried to moan. But of course I hissed instead.

The dog lowered her head and growled. A low, menacing growl. Then she bared her teeth.

I tried to slither away.

Lizzy trailed me. Snarling. Drooling saliva on me.

I slipped under a bush. But she found me. She lowered her head to the ground. I could feel her hot breath on my skin.

With one bite, Lizzy was going to rip the skin off my back. She opened her mouth and —

"Lizzy! Go!" It was Mrs. Gardner. The dog jerked her head up and whimpered.

"Ivan! Come and get the dog. I don't want her in the garden! Ivan!"

No answer.

Mrs. Gardner grabbed Lizzy's collar and tugged the dog inside. I slid out of the bushes and followed right behind.

Mrs. Gardner put the dog in the basement while I slithered up the steps to the bedrooms.

"Lizzy!" I hissed to my friend. I glanced around the room. I spotted the TV. The CD player. The Fruit Bag poster on the wall. But no Lizzy.

And then the light snapped on.

There stood Lizzy in the doorway.

She was here! She would save me!

"Hey, Lizzy!" I cried, twisting my snake body into the air. "Help me! Help me!"

"Yaaaai!" Lizzy screamed. "A snake! Ivan, get in here!"

"No — it's me!" I wanted to shout. But of course I couldn't. What could I do?

Lizzy pressed against the wall as I wriggled over to the remote control on her night table.

I had an idea.

I pushed my head against the power button. The picture flickered on the screen.

So far so good.

I pressed another button until *The Animaniacs* came on. Now she'd understand!

"Ivan — !" Lizzy began. Then she stopped. A light came into her eyes. She did understand! She did! I writhed in happiness.

Lizzy stepped closer. She reached out. She was going to pick me up. To save me!

No! She grabbed hold of her tennis racquet and with a loud cry, swung it hard and whomped me across the room.

Splat! I hit her CD player. My tail struck a button. Fruit Bag began to play.

For a moment, I lay stunned on top of the player, while Lizzy shrieked for Ivan.

Then I got another idea. I began to dance.

"Lizzy!" I hissed. "It's me. It's Jane. I'm dancing the way we always do!"

Lizzy's eyes widened with fear. She cowered in the corner. "Ivan!" she yelled. "Get in here. Now!"

Ivan poked his head in the room. He grinned. "Got a problem?"

"One of your snakes is loose!" Lizzy shrieked. "Get . . . it . . . out . . . of . . . here. NOW!"

"Lizzy," I whimpered. I slinked off the CD player and slithered over to her feet. "You have to save me!"

Lizzy backed into the corner. I coiled around her leg. "Help me!" I hissed.

"Yaaiiii!" she screeched. She hopped on a chair, trying to shake me loose. "Please, Ivan. Take your snake. Take it!"

Ivan strolled over, taking his time. I threw a pleading look up at Lizzy. "Please!" I hissed.

Ivan crouched over me. He stared at me. "It's not my snake," he said. "I don't have any red ones."

Lizzy's voice screeched. "I don't care!" she shouted. "Just get it off of me!"

"All right. All right." Ivan said. He unwrapped me from Lizzy's leg and carried me to his bedroom.

Then he dumped me into his snake cage.

With two other snakes. Their fangs gleamed in

the light. Their hot snake breath washed over me.

I pressed myself against the cage. But they slinked closer and closer.

They know, I thought. They know I'm not a real snake like they are. And they're going to kill me!

They writhed forward — one on each side of me. Hissing. Hissing. They were going to surround me. And attack.

Their long tongues slid out. They darted forward with a sharp jerk and —

Ivan reached into the cage and pulled me out.

"You know, Lizzy," Ivan said, carrying me back into Lizzy's room. "There's something weird about this snake. It's got something on its stomach."

He flipped me over. Then he gasped. "Wow!" he said. "It looks like a zipper! A tiny zipper."

He shoved me into Lizzy's face.

"GET THAT THING OUT OF HERE!" she screeched.

"I mean it, Lizzy. Look! Let's try to unzip it." Ivan set me gently on the floor. He hesitated. Pulled back. Changed his mind again.

Then he took a deep breath, reached down, and tugged on the zipper.

RRRRRIPPPP!

I exploded into my full human body.

Ivan gasped. Lizzy screamed.

"Cool!" Ivan said, reaching over to touch me.

Lizzy kept screaming.

"Hey! How did you do that?" he asked.

My whole body shook as I told them the terrible story.

When I left to go home, Lizzy was still screaming.

A few days later, Lizzy and I sat out on the field. I had just finished practicing.

"That was awesome, Jane," Lizzy said. "That's the highest I've ever seen you jump."

I felt really proud. My jumping was totally excellent today. Yesterday too.

I hopped over to her.

She reached down and petted my soft white fur. "You're going to be the state high-jump champ," she said.

My pink nose twitched. "You're right," I said. "Did you bring any carrots?"

I had to admit it. Lizzy had been right back at that weird store. Those bunny slippers were *definitely* cool!

THE PERFECT SCHOOL

Going to boarding school was not my idea of a great time. It was not my idea at all.

Whose idea was it? My parents', of course.

I knew I was doomed the day the brochure for the Perfect Boarding School arrived in the mail. The slogan on the cover read: Why Settle for Anything Less Than Perfect?

"Perfect" is my parents' favorite word.

Unfortunately, they have me — Brian O'Connor — for a kid. And I'm far from perfect. I make my bed — sometimes. I take a shower — sometimes. I get my homework done — sometimes.

And I please my parents — never.

Before I knew what was happening, my mom and dad had signed me up for the two-week course. On the way to the train station, I begged. I promised to cut back on TV and video games. I promised I wouldn't tease the dog. I even swore I wouldn't eat three Snickers bars for lunch anymore.

But it was no use. They hustled me onto the train and told me to watch for the Perfect van when I got off at the Rockridge Station.

I found a seat across the aisle from a kid who appeared as unhappy as I felt. He was reading something I'd seen before. The brochure from Perfect.

"So what do you think of the place?" I asked.

"I think it stinks!" he snarled. He threw the brochure down on the train floor. "Perfect. Ha! How about a school to teach parents how to be perfect instead?"

"I'd send mine," I agreed. "I'm Brian. My parents are sending me to Perfect, too."

"I'm C.J. So why did your parents send you for training? What did you do?"

"It's more what I didn't do," I explained. "They're always telling me I didn't do this or I forgot to do that. Man, I wake up five minutes late, and the first thing I hear is that I didn't go to bed early enough, and that's why I can't wake up!"

We complained about our parents until the train man called out "Rockridge Station! Rockridge!"

I grabbed my duffel bag and followed C.J. to the door. "Here goes nothing," I muttered.

About half an hour later, the van pulled through the tall iron gates leading to the school. The driver parked near a row of kids standing behind a sign that said PERFECT GRADUATES.

These kids were *weird*. Their line was ruler straight. Each kid wore a gray uniform. Each kid stood straight up and faced forward. Each kid held a gray suitcase in his left hand.

They stood in silence waiting for their parents to pick them up.

Is that what my parents want me to turn out like? I asked myself. If it is, they can forget it right now.

The driver slid open the side door of the van. Another man stood next to him. "I am the director of the Perfect Boarding School," the new guy told us. "Line up in order of height. Tallest at the back. Shortest at the front. Leave your bags in the van. You won't be needing them here."

The director pointed to the first kid in line. "You are number one-twelve," he stated. He gave a number to each of us. I got 116.

"Your instructors will call you by number," the director explained. "You will call each other by number. You will call me and your teachers 'Guardian.' "

How am I going to make it through two weeks at this place? I thought. This guy is nuts!

A car pulled up in front of the other line. The director hurried over to present the parents with their perfect child — and get his envelope of money in return.

Were any of those kids like me when they got here? I wondered. What did the *Guardians* do to change them? What will they do to me? A shiver raced down my back.

Those kids were like robots. Robots!

Four more Guardians waited for us inside the door. One of them tapped me on the shoulder. "Follow me," he said in a low voice. He led me down a hallway and up a flight of stairs.

I caught sight of C.J. going into a room on the first floor. "See you later — " I started to call.

"No talking," the Guardian barked. At the top of the stairs, he turned left. A half-open door clicked shut as we passed it.

What are they trying to hide? I wondered. Why is every single door shut? Why don't they want us talking to each other?

The Guardian ushered me into the last room in the hall. "You will wear the clothing in the drawer. You will eat the meal on the tray. You will wait here until you are summoned," he ordered me. Then he shut the door.

I checked it — locked, of course.

I studied my new room. It didn't take long. There was a single bed with a small dresser on one side. A table with one chair on the other.

I wandered over to the dresser and opened the drawers. Only boring stuff. Gray uniforms, toothpaste, towels.

May as well check out the food, I decided. A

bowl of bumpy gray stuff sat on the table. I scooped up a little with my finger and licked it off. Tasted sort of like oatmeal.

Then I heard something. A rustling noise. From the heating vent near the floor.

The hairs on the back of my neck prickled. Is something down there?

I stretched out on the floor and pressed my ear against the vent. The rustling grew louder.

Not rustling, I realized. Whispering.

"Is someone down there?" I called softly.

The whispering grew louder. What were they saying?

"Can you hear me?" I asked.

"No talking," a Guardian called from down the hall.

The whispering stopped.

What was that? Did I hear voices from another room? Or was someone hiding down there between the walls?

No. That was impossible.

Right?

I was happy to find C.J. in my first training session. I wanted to ask him if he'd heard anyone whispering in the walls. "Hey, C.J.," I said softly.

"No talking," the Guardian in charge of our class ordered. "You will answer each question in the workbook on your desk."

How can he expect us to answer every question?

This thing is more than a hundred pages long. I flipped open the workbook.

Huh? I thought. These questions are strange: "What do you call your parents?" "What is your favorite food?" "What costumes have you worn for Halloween the last five years?"

Why did the Guardians want to know all this stuff? They already knew way too much about me.

So maybe I could confuse them a little. "I call my father Featherhead and my mother Jellyface," I wrote. "My favorite food is lumpy gray oatmeal. Every single Halloween, I've dressed up as a three-humped camel."

I tapped C.J. on the shoulder and held up my workbook so he could read my answers. C.J. snickered.

A strong hand grabbed my shoulder. Hard. "Number one-sixteen, you are a distraction to the others. You will be placed in the Special Training Course."

The Guardian marched me to the front of the room and hit a small buzzer underneath his desk. Another Guardian appeared at the classroom door.

"Take one-sixteen to the Pattern Room," the first Guardian ordered. "His training is being speeded up."

As the second Guardian herded me out the door, I glanced back at C.J. "Sorry," he whispered.

My mouth felt dry as I followed the Guardian

through the hallways. I tried to swallow, but I couldn't. I didn't know what the Special Training Course was — but I definitely didn't want to be in it.

The Guardian stopped in front of a wooden bench where a little girl sat swinging her feet. "Wait here," he ordered, then left.

As soon as the Guardian turned the corner, the girl leaned over to me. "Do you know what they're going to do?" she whispered. "I heard — "

A Guardian opened the door across the hall and called the girl inside. I slumped back against the wall. I was never going to find out what was going on in this creepy place.

I sighed and closed my eyes. Then I heard the whispering again. It was coming from the wall behind my head.

The whispers grew stronger. I pressed my ear against the wall. "Careful. Don't go in the Pattern Room," a voice cried.

My heartbeat thudded in my ears. "Why? What's in the room? Who are you?" I demanded.

"Don't go — "

The door to the Pattern Room opened. A Guardian ordered me inside.

I felt my legs trembling. I hoped the Guardian couldn't tell how scared I was. Slowly I stepped inside the room.

It looked like my doctor's office: a scale, an examining table, a counter with some cotton, bandages, and stuff.

"Step on the scale," the Guardian instructed. Maybe this won't be so bad, I thought.

The Guardian entered my height and weight into his handheld computer. Then he looped a tape measure around my head and recorded the information. He measured every part of my body, down to my toes. He even measured my tongue.

Why does he need all these measurements? I couldn't think of anything he could use them for. Did my special training take some special equipment that fit me exactly?

I remembered a movie my teacher showed in science class. Some scientists hooked wires up to a mouse and then dropped it into a maze. Every time it made a wrong turn, they gave the mouse a shock.

Maybe that's what the Guardians were going to do to me. Maybe they would give me a shock every time I did something my parents wouldn't like.

The Guardian picked up a color wheel from the counter. He held it up to my eyes, trying to find a color that exactly matched.

I felt more confused then ever. When the Guardian had recorded every detail about me, he sent me back to my room. Without a Guardian escort!

I had to find a way to escape. I paused at each

door and listened for voices. I didn't hear anything behind the fourth door. I opened it.

An empty office. With a phone. Yes!

I grabbed it and dialed my home number. The phone rang once. Please answer, Mom, I silently begged. Two rings. Three rings. Four rings.

I heard footsteps approaching the door. Answer. Answer.

Five rings.

"Hello?" my mom said breathlessly.

"Mom!" I whispered. "You have to get me out of this place! Something weird is going on here. I'm scared."

"Brian, you just got there yesterday. Give it a chance," Mom replied impatiently.

"But they — "

A cold hand pulled the phone away from me. I spun around. The director stood behind me.

"Hello, Mrs. O'Connor," he said. "This is the school Director. Your son Brian will be ready early. Truly special children often finish our program before the others. Yes. First thing tomorrow will be fine."

The director hung up the phone and marched me up to my room. "You have made your last error," he told me as he shut the door behind him.

What is that supposed to mean? I wondered. Are they still planning to give me the special training? Or are they sending me home — *un*perfect?

I flopped down on the bed. Every time I heard

footsteps in the hall, I thought a Guardian had arrived to take me for training.

I guess I finally dropped off to sleep. I had a dream about looking for my dog at the pound. All the dogs were whimpering.

When I woke up, the whimpering continued.

I jumped up and scrambled over to the vent. I peered down. Far below me, I saw dozens of glittering eyes.

"Save us!" a voice cried. "Save us — and yourself."

"Robots," another voice whispered. "The school makes a robot of you. They send home the robot in your place. A perfect robot. And then they make you live down here where no one can ever find you."

So *that's* why the Guardians asked those questions and took so many measurements! They were making a robot of me to send home to Mom and Dad!

My whole body trembled. I could barely breathe. "What do I do?" I demanded. "How can I — ?"

"Shhh. Someone's coming," another voice warned.

The eyes disappeared back into the darkness.

I had to get out of my room — now. I tore a piece of paper off the sheet lining one of the dresser drawers. Then I knocked lightly on the door. No answer. I knocked a little louder.

"Yes?" a Guardian called.

"I need to go to the bathroom," I said.

He opened the door. As I passed through, I shoved the paper into the lock.

The Guardian escorted me to the bathroom and then returned me to my room. He shut the door firmly behind him.

I waited a few minutes. Then I tried the door. It opened. The paper kept the door from locking!

I grabbed my spoon from the table and opened the door a crack. When the Guardian was looking in the opposite direction, I hurled the spoon down the hall as far as I could.

The Guardian heard the clattering sound and turned toward it. I slipped out of my room and ran down the hall the other way.

So far so good. I crept down the stairs.

"What are you doing down here?" someone demanded.

"N-nothing," I stuttered. Then my eyes adjusted to the dark hallway. "C.J., it's you!" I was so glad to see him! "We've got to get out of this school — now!" I told him.

His eyes bulged in surprise. "Huh?"

"There are kids trapped behind the walls. We have to save them — and us!" I exclaimed, tugging his hand.

"Follow me," C.J. answered. "I know where to go."

C.J. grabbed my arm and led me around the

corner and down a short hallway. He pressed on a wall panel — and it slid open.

"Quick. In here," he whispered. "It leads outside."

"Great!" I cried. I ducked my head and started into the narrow opening.

To my surprise, I saw only darkness. And heard whispering voices. Shuffling feet.

"Hey — !" I spun around to C.J. "This doesn't lead outside!" I protested. "This is where all the kids are hidden!"

"Sorry," C.J. replied in a cold, low voice. "This is where you will be hidden too, Brian. I work for the Guardians. My job was to guard you."

"No!" I shrieked. "No! Let me out! Let me out!"

But to my horror, the wall panel began to slide shut behind me.

"Thank you very much, Director," my mother said. "Brian looks perfect."

She admired my gray uniform, my perfectly brushed hair, my perfect smile. I stood straight as an arrow. I faced forward as a good robot should. I held the gray suitcase in my left hand, as all of the robots are programmed.

My mother shook hands with the Director. She handed him an envelope filled with money.

"He will be perfect now," the Director said. "We guarantee it."

That was two days ago. And I'm trying to be as perfect as I can be.

Because I don't want anyone to catch on.

It wasn't easy to pull C.J. into the dark chamber and escape before the wall closed up. And it wasn't easy to sneak into the robot room. To grab my robot and drag it up to my room. And then to sneak back into the robot room and pretend to be a robot.

Yes, I don't want anyone to catch on that the *real* Brian O'Connor came home. I don't want anyone to know that I escaped.

Some day soon I'm going back to that place and rescue those poor kids. But right now I'm being as perfect as I can be.

Okay, okay.

So I teased the dog this morning. And ate three Snickers bars for lunch. And spilled some grape juice on the white couch in the den.

But other than that, I've been perfect.

Really.

FOR THE BIRDS

"We're here!" Dad announced happily. "Happy vacation, everyone!"

Some vacation! I grumbled to myself.

My family piled out of the car. All five of us. I stretched my legs after the long ride. Then I gazed up at the lodge.

What a dump.

It looked like the log cabin on the maple syrup bottle. Except it was falling apart.

A log hung over the door with words carved into it: WELCOME TO BIRD HAVEN LODGE.

It should be called Bird *Brain* Lodge! I told myself, rolling my eyes. Only a birdbrain would come to a place like this!

Mom gave Dad's arm a squeeze. "Oh, Henry! It's so romantic!"

Romantic? Okay, maybe I'm only twelve. Maybe I don't think much about romantic stuff. But that wasn't exactly the word that came to my mind.

The word that came to my mind was *stupid*!

"Can't we go to a *real* hotel?" I pleaded for the thousandth time.

But Mom and Dad were too busy smooching to answer. They always acted this way on their wedding anniversary — which was today.

"Move it, Kim," ordered my fifteen-year-old brother, Ben. He had on his favorite T-shirt. It said: *So many birds, so little time!*

Do you believe it? A fifteen-year-old boy who's into bird-watching?

"Yeah, move it, Kim," echoed my other brother, Andy. He's thirteen. His hair hangs down over his eyes. I can never tell if he's looking at me. "We want to do some bird-watching before dark."

To me, if you've seen one bird, you've seen them all. But everybody else in my family is bird crazy! They spend all their time in the woods, staring through binoculars.

And if they spot a new bird to check off on their list, they go totally nuts.

It's sick. That's the only way to describe it.

And now here we are at Bird Haven Lodge. A whole week of bird-watching, bird talk — nothing but birds all the time.

Thrills and chills, huh?

Carrying my suitcase, I started up the gravel path to the lodge. Tall hedges lined the path on both sides. The hedges were trimmed into bird shapes. I passed what looked like a leafy pigeon. Then an eagle. I brushed by a bushy duck about ten feet tall.

"I'm going to hurl. Really," I complained.

My family pretended they didn't hear me. I guess they were sick of my complaints. But what was I supposed to do while they crawled through the trees gawking at birds?

"Check it out!" exclaimed Andy as we reached the lodge. "A pair of great horned owls!"

"No way," Ben scoffed. "Those are screech owls."

"Owls in the daytime?" I asked. "Where?"

"Right there, stupid," Ben said, pointing.

Then I saw them. They were standing guard on either side of the steps. Owls carved out of hedges.

Big deal — right?

"We're the Petersons," Dad told the big, jolly-looking man at the check-in desk.

"I've been expecting you," the man replied with a big smile. "I'm Mr. Dove."

"Mr. *Dove*?" I mumbled. "Give me a break!"

Mr. Dove's round, little bird eyes darted from Mom to Dad. "Mr. and Mrs. Peterson," he said, "you'll be in the Lovebird Suite."

Mr. Dove ran his fingers down the register. "Now . . . let . . . me . . . see. I have a double for the boys on the third floor in the Blue Jay Wing." Mr. Dove eyed me. "And for you — the Cuckoo's Nest."

"Cuckoo!" Ben and Andy hooted. "Cuckoo Kim!"

I shot Mr. Dove a dirty look. But he didn't seem to notice.

"Follow me," he said. "I'll show you to your rooms."

We followed him down the hall to the Lovebird Suite.

"These doors lead out to a terrace with an old-fashioned swing," Mr. Dove practically cooed. "Would you like to see it now?"

But Mom and Dad were too busy smooching to answer.

Uh-hmmm. Mr. Dove cleared his throat.

Mom giggled. "We can see the terrace later," she said. "Come on, Henry. Let's go see the kids' rooms."

We took the elevator up to the third floor. Ben and Andy dashed into their room, snatched binoculars from their backpacks, and ran outside to spot some birds.

"Now to Cuckoo's Nest," Mr. Dove announced.

"I'm the only one here who *isn't* cuckoo!" I muttered. I don't think anyone heard me.

Mom and Dad and I followed Mr. Dove again. We turned down a narrow hallway. We kept walking. And walking. We didn't see any other guests.

"Um, where *is* my room, anyway?" I asked.

"We're almost there," Mr. Dove sang out.

When we reached the far end of the hall, he stopped and opened a door.

"How unusual!" Mom exclaimed, stepping into the room.

Mom had *that* right. Cuckoo's Nest was small. Tiny, actually. And it was round. A round room.

"I don't know . . ." I began. "It's, um, so *far* from everybody."

"Don't be silly, Kim," Mom said. "It's a lovely little nest!"

I groaned. "Mom — can't you stop with the bird talk for one second? I'm sick of birds! Sick of them!"

I saw Mr. Dove staring at me, surprised by my sudden outburst.

Dad walked over to a window. "What a view!" he exclaimed. "Kim, you can see right into the famous Mockingbird Maze."

I joined Dad at the window. The maze looked like one out of my old *Pencil Fun and Games* book. Except that this maze was made out of twelve-foot-tall hedges. It went round and round and round. It seemed to have a hundred different dead ends.

I'd hate to get lost in there, I thought. "Hey!" I exclaimed. "There are Ben and Andy — inside the maze!"

Mr. Dove frowned. "You should save the maze

for tomorrow," he told Mom and Dad. "You'll need a full day to do it right."

"Why don't you go outside too, Kim?" Dad suggested. "Your mother and I have some unpacking to do."

Well, I went downstairs. But I didn't go outside. I don't really like to be outdoors at all. Too many birds.

I wandered around the lodge. I thought maybe I'd find someone else my age. Or a game room. Or a TV to watch.

But the place was empty.

Finally I sat down on a low couch in a room near the front desk. I guess it was some kind of rec room. I stared at the stone fireplace for a while. There were stuffed birds all around it on the wall. Pheasants and ducks and owls. Yuck!

I picked up an old magazine and settled back against the couch.

"Oww!" I cried out as a sharp pain shot up my back.

I jumped to my feet. A picture flashed into my mind. A huge, angry bird — a hawk or a falcon. It had dug its sharp beak into my back!

I spun around — and gazed down at a pair of hedge clippers.

"Huh?" I picked them up. Heavy, metal hedge clippers. I hadn't even seen them when I sat down on them.

I turned to see Mr. Dove enter the room. "You found them!" he cried. A smile crossed his round face. He hurried over to me. "Thank you! I've been searching all over for these!"

"I — I sat on them," I stammered. I handed them to him.

"I'm so grateful you found them." He beamed at me. "I owe you a big favor, Kim."

"No. Really — " I started.

"I owe you a favor," he insisted. His smile faded. "I guess you'd like revenge."

"Excuse me?" I thought I hadn't heard correctly.

"Revenge against your family. For bringing you here," he said, smiling again.

"Uh . . . no. That's okay," I replied uncertainly. "I'm . . . uh . . . enjoying it." I hurried out of the room. "Bye."

What did he mean by that? I wondered. He's just like my family, I finally decided. Totally nuts.

That night, we ate in the hotel dining room. I hoped to see some other kids at dinner. Some *normal* kids. Kids who couldn't tell a red hawk from a turkey buzzard. But we were the only ones in the dining room.

Mr. Dove was our waiter. Maybe he was the cook, too. Did anyone else work here? I wondered.

Ben and Andy couldn't stop talking about how

many birds they'd seen. They were so excited. "There are *thousands* of birds here!" Andy declared.

"No. Millions!" Ben corrected him.

Mom and Dad held hands all through dinner. They couldn't wait for us all to explore Mockingbird Maze in the morning.

I tuned out. I'd never been so bored in all my life.

Later, I was in my room, trying to get to sleep. I closed my eyes. I listened to the wind blow through the trees. I tossed and turned for hours. I twisted my covers into knots. No way could I fall asleep in Cuckoo's Nest.

The wind began to pick up. I heard flapping. Must be the awnings over the windows, I thought.

Then I heard a cry. My eyes popped open. I glanced around the room. It was flooded with moonlight. Shadows flitted on the bed, the floor, everywhere.

I threw back the covers and tiptoed over to a window.

I gasped!

The sky was thick with birds!

They circled in front of my room. Cawing and cackling.

An enormous crow landed on my ledge.

It stared at me with its bottomless, black-hole eyes. Then it pecked at the glass.

It's trying to tell me something, I thought.

A weird thought. But the whole thing was so weird. Why were the birds flying at night? Why were they circling in front of me? Cawing and chirping so demandingly?

They really did seem as if they were trying to communicate.

With a shudder, I pulled the curtain, hurried back to bed and slept with two pillows over my head.

The next morning, Andy and Ben woke me up at dawn. They insisted that I come with the family into Mockingbird Maze.

"I might as well," I said, yawning. "There's nothing else to do here." That was as enthusiastic as I could get.

The five of us ate a hurried breakfast. Then, armed with notebooks, bird books, and binoculars, we stepped out into a gray morning. The sun hadn't climbed over the trees. The morning dew still glistened on the grass.

What am I *doing* here? I asked myself, shaking my head unhappily. I hate birds. I *hate* them!

To our surprise, we found Mr. Dove at the entrance to the maze. He wore blue denim overalls, and he carried the hedge clippers. His round face was red and sweaty. I guess he had gotten an early start pruning in the maze.

"Good morning, everyone." He grinned at me. "I hope you enjoy the maze. Lots to see. Lots of surprises."

He chatted with Mom and Dad for a few minutes. Andy and Ben started chirping at me. "Cuckoo! Cuckoo! Cuckoo Kim!" They think they're a riot, but they're just dumb.

A short while later, we stepped into the maze. The tall hedges cast dark shadows over the path. I already felt lost!

We took about five steps — and stopped.

"Oh, wow!" I cried out. Standing in front of us was a huge hedge sculpture. Five people carved out of hedge. And the five people were *us*!

"Mr. Dove — !" Dad called. "What *is* this?"

We turned to see him grinning at us from the maze entrance. He waved the big hedge clippers. "All part of the program," he called. "Part of the program." He disappeared.

Dad shook his head. "What an odd bird," he muttered.

"Dad — *please!*" I begged. "Stop with the bird talk!"

We admired the hedge portrait for a while. I'm not sure why, but it gave me the creeps. Why did Mr. Dove do it? What did he mean, it was part of the program?

The questions repeated in my mind as we made our way through the twisting maze. Everyone else oohed and aahed over all the birds. There were hundreds of them. All different kinds. All chirping and cawing and crowing at once.

I had to hold my hands over my ears. It was deafening!

These birds are all chirping at once because they're trying to tell us something. That thought flashed through my mind again. That's totally crazy, I told myself. And I pushed the thought out of my head.

I shouldn't have.

I should have paid attention to my growing fear.

But now it was too late.

We stepped into a narrow tunnel — and came out the other end into a round structure. Dome-shaped. Made of metal wires.

It took us a few seconds to realize we had stepped into a cage. A giant bird cage.

"Wow — this is awesome!" Andy declared.

"What a great maze!" Ben agreed.

Then the wire door snapped shut behind us.

Andy's smile vanished. "Hey — how do we get out?" he cried.

"You can fly out," a voice replied. Mr. Dove appeared from a trapdoor in the cage floor.

"Huh? What do you mean?" Mom cried. She grabbed Dad's arm. "What's going on, Mr. Dove?"

"All part of the program," Mr. Dove replied. "All part of the program. I want you to be happy birds."

"Excuse me? Happy *birds*?" I demanded.

"It's a very old trick I learned," Mr. Dove said. "Quite easy. If you get the hedge sculpture right. Quite easy. And now you can join your feathered friends. You'll be happy. I want you to be happy."

Before we could say anything, Mr. Dove raised the hedge clippers. He pointed them at Mom and Dad. And clicked the blades together twice.

"Nooooo!" I wailed as I watched Mom and Dad shrink away — change shape — and flutter up against the cage wall.

"I turned them into lovebirds." Mr. Dove beamed. "Now they'll be happy."

"Noooo!" Another horrified wail escaped my throat as the hedge clippers clicked twice more. And as I stared in shock, not believing it, not believing it — but seeing it — my brothers were also changed into fluttering, chirping birds.

"Two mockingbirds," Mr. Dove said. "They'll like that."

He turned to me.

"No — please!" I begged. "Please don't turn me into a bird! Please!"

He smiled. "Of course not, Kim. I owe you a favor. I know you hate birds — right?"

"Please — !" I repeated. "Please — !"

"I said I'd help you pay them back," he said softly.

"No. Please — !" I begged. "Please don't — "

My family chirped and twittered, fluttering across the cage excitedly.

"I want you to be happy, Kim," Mr. Dove said.

Then he clicked the hedge clippers and changed me, too.

He changed me into — a cat.

ALIENS IN THE GARDEN

Thick, black clouds rolled across the sky as I walked toward the park. Lightning flashed and thunder rumbled in the distance.

Forget the park, Kurt, I told myself. Nobody will show up in this weather, anyway.

More thunder. Louder now. That did it. I turned around and started for home. As I hurried around the corner, I spotted Rocky up ahead of me.

I stopped — and wished I could disappear.

Rocky is a dog. A mean, vicious dog with ratty brown fur, sharp yellow fangs, and killer eyes.

I held my breath and crossed my fingers that he wouldn't come any closer. And I got lucky. Rocky sniffed in the gutter for a couple of seconds, then trotted away.

I let my breath out in a big whoosh.

"Yo, Creep-o!" a voice roared from behind me.

I sucked in my breath again. "I should have

known," I mumbled. Wherever Rocky goes, Flip won't be far behind.

Slowly, I turned around and faced him.

Flip is Rocky's owner. Flip is fourteen, two years older than I am. And he's huge, with the same ratty hair and yellow teeth as his dog.

It's hard to decide which one is meaner.

"Where do you think you're going, Kurt?" he demanded.

"Home," I told him. "A storm is coming."

"Ooh, a storm!" He sneered and pushed me backwards. "Gonna go hide under the bed?"

Flip's favorite sport is picking on me. He pushed me again, harder. I almost fell. "Get a life, Flip!" I yelled. "Go sniff gutters with your mutt!"

Flip's eyes narrowed. He clenched his big fists. You should have kept your mouth shut, I told myself. You're in major trouble now!

Just as Flip dove for me, a shaft of lightning split the clouds. Thunder boomed. More lightning flashed, and then rain poured out of the sky.

"Aah, you're not worth getting soaked for," Flip growled. Instead of pounding me to dust, he shoved me aside and took off.

Saved by a summer storm! I'd lucked out after all.

Upstairs in my bedroom, I changed into dry clothes. I could hear the wind howling outside. I ran to the window and crouched down in front of it to watch the storm. As I did, I saw something whiz past outside. Another lightning bolt split the sky. It zapped the flying object and lit it up.

I stared hard at the object. It looked like a toy spaceship.

I mashed my nose against the windowpane to see better. There! It hovered low over the backyard garden. Wobbling back and forth. Out of control.

I craned my neck to watch. The object spiraled down . . . down . . . down . . . then — *splat*! It nose-dived right into the middle of a berry bush.

I kept my eyes on that bush until the storm finally blew itself out. It wasn't a long storm, but it was one of the heaviest I've ever seen. When the rain slowed to a drizzle, I ran outside and sloshed my way into the garden.

Disaster area! Ripped leaves and broken branches covered the ground. Slimy green vegetable guts dripped down the fence. Mud slithered into my shoes and oozed between my toes.

I squished over to the berry bush and stooped down. Bloodred juice splattered onto my fingers as I pried some branches apart.

There sat the object, stuck nose-first into the ground under the bush. Wisps of hissing steam rose up from it.

I cautiously reached down and touched it.

Warm, but not too hot. The mud made a sucking sound as I tugged it loose.

I wiped the object on my shirt and stared at it.

Some kind of spaceship, for sure. Made out of metal. Cone-shaped, with three little wings at one end and a tinted window at the other. I couldn't see inside.

But it's definitely not a toy, I decided. It's too solid. And it survived the storm *and* the crash.

An awesome thought suddenly hit me. Could the little spaceship be real?

I always figured flying saucers and alien spaceships had to be huge. But I'd never seen one. How could I know for sure that I didn't have one in my hands?

I tucked the ship under my arm and hurried to the park to show it to my best friend, Jenna. I knew she would show up. Jenna loves going to the park. She practically lives there.

As I sat down on a bench, Flip burst out of some bushes and landed in front of me. Guess my luck ran out.

"Hey, Creep-o, what's that?" he asked, grabbing for the spaceship.

I tried to push him away, but he yanked me straight off the bench and tossed me into the grass.

The ship flew from my hand and landed nearby.

Flip stared at it. His mouth hung open for a

second. Then he shook his ratty head and bellowed out a laugh. "A toy spaceship? Aren't you a little old to be playing with toys?"

As I struggled to my knees, Flip reached for the ship. I knew he'd try to smash it, so I made a grab for it.

In a flash, Flip had me in a headlock. His arm squeezed tighter around my neck. I tried to pull it away. The muscle felt like a stone. His arm didn't budge.

I gasped for air.

Flip let out another laugh.

But his laugh turned into a shriek. To my surprise, his arm dropped from my neck.

I sank to the ground. Flip shrieked again.

I sucked in air and stared up at him.

He held his face with one hand and hopped up and down, screeching in pain.

As I gazed at him, a blue light zipped past my eyes and hit Flip on his bony knee. Sparks flew from his skin. He roared and dropped to the ground. Then he rolled over, leaped up, and ran off.

Saved again! I thought. But by what? Where did that blue light come from?

I sat up and glanced around.

And gasped.

On the ground near the ship stood three small aliens.

Aliens? You're seeing things, Kurt, I told myself. Flip's choke-hold cut off your air and messed up your brain.

I glanced away. Shook my head to clear it. Blinked hard and rubbed my eyes. Slowly, I glanced back at the ground.

The aliens still stood there, not much taller than the grass. They wore puffy silver suits and round white helmets with shaded visors.

Whoa! Not only had a real spaceship crashed into the garden, but it had real aliens in it. Awesome!

I stared hard — and saw that each alien clutched a tiny gun in its hand.

Ray guns. Ray guns that shot a painful blue light!

I'm toast now! I thought, jumping to my feet.

But instead of zapping me, the aliens shoved the guns into their suits. Then they tilted their heads way back and gazed up at me.

I crouched down on my hands and knees. I stuck my face real close to one of the aliens and squinted into its visor.

A weird face with bright-red hair growing all over it. Beady little eyes. A button nose and a smile on its tiny mouth.

I heard a faint squeaking sound. I stared harder. The alien's lips flapped. It's talking! I realized. An alien is actually talking to me!

I grinned. "Hi, I'm Kurt," I told it. "Listen, thanks for zapping Flip."

All three aliens grabbed their helmets and cringed.

At first I didn't get it. Then I realized the problem — my voice. I'm at least a hundred times as big as these little guys, I told myself. My voice is killing their ears.

"Flip is a total bully," I whispered. "I really owe you one. I mean, you saved my life!"

I peered at the first alien again. It just shook its head and shrugged. It couldn't understand a word I said.

"Hey, Kurt what are you doing?" a voice called out from behind me. My friend Jenna's voice. The aliens stood still as she dropped onto the ground beside me.

Jenna gazed at the aliens. Then she slowly glanced at me. "Please tell me you're not playing with dolls, Kurt."

"They're not dolls," I whispered. "They're aliens."

"Alien what?"

"Alien aliens," I told her. "From outer space."

She rolled her eyes. "Give me a break!"

"Keep your voice down!" I whispered. "It hurts their ears."

"You're kidding, right?" Jenna glanced at the aliens. "Hello down there!" she cried.

The aliens grabbed their heads and cringed again.

Jenna gasped. Her green eyes grew huge.

"Kurt!" she whispered. "Please tell me you've got a remote control somewhere."

I pulled the pockets of my shorts inside out. "No remote, Jenna."

"This is unreal!" she murmured. But I could tell she believed me now. "How did they get here?"

I pointed to the ship. "The storm knocked it out of the sky, into my garden."

"Wow!" Jenna gazed at the aliens. "I never thought I'd see anything like this! I mean, there's actually life on another planet somewhere!" She bent lower and squinted closely at the first alien.

"Don't make any sudden moves," I warned. "It's got a mean ray gun. They all do. Flip tried to choke me — and they zapped him."

Jenna grinned. "If they zapped Flip, they're definitely good guys." She inspected the alien again. "I wonder where they're from."

"I don't know, but I bet they want to go home," I told her.

"After meeting Flip, who wouldn't?" Jenna muttered. "Can the ship still fly?"

Before I could answer, the aliens suddenly stiffened.

I glanced up. "Uh-oh! Flip's back!" I warned. "And he brought Drake along for company!"

Flip and his cousin Drake were tearing along the path toward the bench. Drake carried a bat. With a wild laugh, Flip vaulted the bench and landed near the spaceship.

The aliens scattered.

"Ready for some fun?" Flip roared to Drake.

Drake snickered.

"Leave them alone!" I shouted.

Flip laughed again. "Hey, Creep-o, didn't your mother ever teach you to share your toys!"

Two of the aliens scurried off in opposite directions. Drake darted after one of them, whacking his bat on the ground and laughing.

"Cut it out!" Jenna cried. She chased after Drake.

I spotted the third alien running for the ship. It tripped over a twig and fell on its face.

Flip snatched it up in his fat hand. "You're dog meat!" he snarled at it.

He pinned the alien's arms to its sides and began to squeeze.

He'll squash it! I thought. They saved me. Now it was my turn to save them!

I made a desperate leap. I crashed against Flip's knees, knocking him to the ground. The alien popped from his hand and tumbled end over end through the air.

I stretched my arms out as far as I could and caught it inches from the ground. It struggled to its feet on my palm.

"Kurt's got one!" Flip shouted to Drake, scrambling up. "Forget the others. Get Kurt!"

Drake and Flip charged at me. Jenna jumped on Flip's back, but he shook her off easily.

I slipped the alien into the pocket of my shorts — and ran!

I dashed along the path, scuttled through some bushes and into a clearing. As I sprinted up a grassy hill, I heard Flip and Drake crashing through the bushes after me.

I put on more speed and charged down the other side of the hill. Then I doubled back.

Gasping for breath, I crawled through the bushes again. At the edge of the path, I peeked out.

And froze.

Flip's dog, Rocky, stood on the path, his killer eyes glaring straight into mine.

My heart hammered against my chest.

Rocky's lips curled back. His yellow fangs dripped saliva. He lowered his huge, shaggy head and snarled. He pawed the ground. Snarled again.

And sprang at me!

I cried out as a blue light zapped through the air. It caught Rocky right between the eyes!

The dog yelped and dropped to the ground at my feet, looking dazed.

The blue light meant only one thing — an alien close by. I glanced around and spotted it, caught in a thicket of thorny branches.

"Thanks again!" I whispered, reaching into the bush. The tiny spacesuit ripped as I tugged the alien free. I quickly dropped it into my other pocket.

Still dazed, Rocky whined meekly as I stepped past him and bolted down the path.

"Kurt!" Jenna cried when she saw me. "Hurry!"

"I've got two of the aliens!" I gasped, running up to her. "We've got to find the other one!"

"I did," she told me. "It's in the ship. Maybe it's trying to get the spaceship working."

"Let's hope it can." I dug the other two aliens out of my pockets and set them in the open hatch of the ship.

They waved at me, then hurried inside. The tiny hatch closed.

A loud, angry bark made Jenna and me spin around. Rocky had recovered and was charging toward us. Flip and Drake raced behind him, shouting, "Get the aliens!"

I stooped down next to the spaceship. Tiny red lights flickered on, but it didn't move.

The barking and shouting grew louder.

The spaceship still didn't move.

I had to do something! I grabbed it off the ground, cocked my arm back — and *hurled* the ship as high into the air as I could!

The ship soared upward. Higher . . . higher.

Then the nose dipped.

Jenna and I both gasped.

The spaceship began to spiral down.

Rocky chased after it, barking wildly. Flip and Drake cheered.

I groaned and started to cover my eyes. But

then I saw a puff of smoke from the back of the ship. Then another. The little spacecraft leveled off — and began to climb.

"Yes!" I cheered.

Flip and Drake stared with their mouths hanging open.

More smoke billowed. The red lights twinkled. The ship kept climbing. It rose higher and higher, until all we could see was a silver dot in the sky.

"Unreal!" Jenna kept muttering as we hurried out of the park. "Real, but totally *un*real!"

"Flip and Drake still can't believe it," I said, snickering. "They're both back in the park, gaping at the sky."

She laughed. "Too bad the aliens couldn't have zapped them one last time."

"Yeah, and it's too bad they couldn't have stayed a little longer." I stared up at the sky, too. "One thing is for sure — I'll never forget them."

"I'll bet they never forget *us*, either." Jenna pointed at an ice cream truck down the street. "And I think we deserve a reward for saving them, don't you?"

"Definitely." I dug into my pockets and pulled out some coins.

I also pulled out a tiny scrap of silver material.

"Hey! It's a piece of a spacesuit," I told Jenna. "It must be from the alien that got caught in the thorn bush."

Jenna squinted at the scrap. "It's part of a sleeve, I think. And there's something on it. Something colorful."

We forgot about the ice cream and ran to my house. I found my magnifying glass and peered at the scrap through the lens.

"What do you see?" Jenna asked.

"I'm not sure." I closed one eye to focus better. "It's a rectangle," I told her. "With stripes going across it. Red and white stripes. The upper left-hand corner is blue. And it has a bunch of white stars on it." I counted them. "Fifty stars."

"Weird." Jenna frowned. "I wonder what it means."

"Me, too," I agreed. "Maybe it's some kind of symbol. A flag or something. From the aliens' planet." I sighed. "I guess we'll never know."

"Let's go get that ice cream," Jenna said.

I tucked the tiny cloth rectangle into my pocket and followed her out the door.

THE THUMBPRINT OF DOOM

"Let's go swimming in the lake," I suggested.

"Trisha, you already said that. Can't you think of anything else to do?" Jeremy asked. "Harold doesn't want to go swimming. He's afraid."

I was afraid too. Afraid that this was going to be the most boring summer of my life.

Usually I go to sleep-away camp in the summer — but not this year. This year I thought it would be fun to hang out with my best friend, Jeremy.

I thought wrong.

I didn't know his cousin Harold was visiting — for two whole months. Nerdy Harold. Ugh.

We're all twelve, but Harold seems a lot younger. Probably because he's really, really short. The total opposite of me and Jeremy.

"What are you afraid of, anyway?" I asked Harold, tightening my ponytail. We were walking around the block for the third time, trying to decide what to do.

"Yeah, what *are* you afraid of?" Jeremy asked.

"Fungus."

"What?" Jeremy and I shouted together.

"Fungus," Harold repeated. "You know, those tiny plants that live in the water. The ones that are so small, you can't see them."

"So what about them?" I asked.

"Well, I don't like things I can't see," Harold mumbled.

I'm doomed, I thought, staring at Harold. This really was going to be the worst summer of my life.

"How about the movies?" Jeremy suggested.

Harold said okay, so we headed for town. We had walked halfway down the block when I spotted her.

"Look," I said, turning to Jeremy. "There's the new girl. Her family moved in last week. Mom says she's our age. Let's go say hi."

I stared at the girl as we walked over. She was really pretty. Her long, shiny black hair hung down to her waist, and her skin was a beautiful olive color. She wore khaki shorts and a matching T-shirt.

"Hi!" I called when we reached her yard. "You're my new neighbor. I live over there," I said, pointing out my house.

"I'm Carla," she introduced herself, striding across the lawn in her bare feet. "We just moved in."

Carla glanced at Jeremy, then at Harold. She had the brightest green eyes I'd ever seen.

"I'm Trisha. This is Jeremy and Harold. We're going to the movies," I said. "Want to come?"

"I'd really like to," Carla started. "But I can't. My horoscope says I shouldn't go anywhere today."

"You believe in that stuff?" I asked.

"Well, I'm kind of into it. I'm pretty superstitious."

"You mean you're afraid of black cats and stuff?" Harold asked.

"Harold is only afraid of things he can't see," I told her.

Jeremy shoved his elbow into my side. Carla didn't seem to notice. She continued, "Well, I'm not afraid of black cats. But some things. Have you ever heard of the Thumbprint of Doom?"

"The Thumbprint of Doom?" I repeated. We shook our heads no.

"Well, if someone puts it on your forehead," Carla explained, lowering her voice to a whisper, "you're doomed! Something horrible will happen to you in less than twenty-four hours."

"Do you *really* believe that?" I asked.

"Yes," she replied. "Yes, I do. It's the thing I'm most afraid of."

"We — we have to go," Harold stammered. "We're going to be late for the movie."

"Okay. See you around," Carla said. The three of us hurried away.

"Boy, was she weird," Jeremy snickered.

"Totally," I agreed. Then I waved my arms over my head and started shrieking. "Oooooo! The Thumbprint of Doooooom." I jabbed my thumb onto Jeremy's forehead, hard.

Jeremy chased me down the street trying to give *me* the Thumbprint of Doom. Then we both raced after Harold. We tackled him to the ground and gave him the *Double* Thumbprint of Doom!

The next day, Jeremy and I headed down to the lake to go rowing. Harold decided to stay home — to read the dictionary. He says he wants to finish it by Christmas. He's already up to the *P*'s; I convinced him he was way behind schedule.

"You get in first," I told Jeremy when we reached the lake, "and set up the oars." Jeremy had a hard time slipping the oars into the oarlocks. They were about a hundred years old — rotted and warped.

The old wood creaked and groaned as I slid the boat into the water. I started to jump in — when I heard the scream.

A terrified scream.

"Trisha! Noooooo!"

I lost my balance and fell into the lake.

I fumbled for the side of the boat and pulled

myself up, gasping for air. Then I threw myself on the shore.

"Are you okay?" It was Carla.

I couldn't speak. I nodded.

"Hope I didn't scare you," she said. "But you can't ride a blue canoe on Tuesday!"

"Huh?" Jeremy cried, helping me up.

"It's bad luck," Carla said. "A blue canoe on Tuesday is bad luck for Wednesday."

"Carla, you scared me to death," I sputtered. "I don't believe in those weird superstitions. *And I don't believe you did such a stupid thing,*" I muttered under my breath.

While I wrung out my T-shirt and poured the water from my new sneakers, Carla apologized. Then the three of us headed home. I wanted to be mad at Carla, but I couldn't. She was convinced that she had saved my life.

"Hey! There's Harold," Jeremy pointed out on our way back. Harold was walking down the street, dodging from tree to tree. I'd seen him do that before. He was trying to avoid the dogs — if there were any.

"Hey! Guys! I finished the *P*'s!" He ran up to us. "Isn't that great, Trisha? I finished the *P*'s!" Then he shot his arms out and — he shoved me hard!

I fell to the ground and scraped my knees.

"HAROLD!" I screamed. "What did you do that for?"

"You were going to step on a crack! See," he said, pointing to the sidewalk.

"So what!"

"It's bad luck, Trisha," he explained. "Step on a crack, break your mother's back."

"Since when do you believe in superstitions?" Jeremy asked.

"Since we met Carla," Harold said, smiling at her. "I think she makes a lot of sense."

This was *definitely* going to be the worst summer of my life, I thought.

But I didn't know how right I was.

A few days later, Carla stopped by the baseball field to watch us play.

It was the bottom of the ninth, we were one run behind, and I was up at bat. We already had two outs, so I was really nervous. The game was all up to me.

I planted my feet in the batter's box and waited for the pitch. It flew past me. So did the next one. Two strikes.

"This is it, Trisha," I told myself. "Concentrate!"

My eyes were glued to the ball. It was coming — a fast ball. My favorite pitch!

I started to swing and —

"TRISHHHA!" Carla ran out onto the field. "Don't!" she shrieked, waving her arms high in the air.

The ball whizzed by me. "Strike three!"

"Carla!" I screamed. "What is your *problem*?"

"It's thirteen minutes after one o'clock on Friday the thirteenth," she said in a rush. "You can't hit a ball now. It would be a disaster!"

"Thanks, Carla," I grumbled. "Thanks a lot."

Carla and Harold left right after the game. Jeremy waited for me to collect my stuff from the bench. Then we walked home together.

"I can't take it anymore," I complained. "Do you know what Carla did to me yesterday?"

Jeremy shook his head no.

"She forced me to walk around the fire hydrant seven times — backwards."

"Why?" Jeremy asked.

"I don't know *why*, Jeremy. All I know is she's driving me crazy. Those superstitions are ruining my life."

Jeremy shrugged.

"We've got to show Carla that superstitions are totally dumb, Jeremy. We've got to. The question is *how*?"

Three days later, I knew how. I had a plan to cure Carla of her superstitions forever. It was sneaky. But it was good.

Friday night after dinner, Jeremy, Harold, and I stopped by her house.

"We're riding over to the Jefferson Field fairgrounds," I told her. "To check out the new carnival. You've got to come!"

Carla stood in the doorway, holding open the screen door. "Tonight?" She narrowed her eyes. Thinking. "No," she finally said. "Not tonight. The stars aren't right."

We begged and pleaded, and finally dragged her out of the house.

By the time we reached the fairgrounds, the sun had set. Jefferson Field sparkled in the dark with thousands of colored lights. They decorated a huge Ferris wheel. And a giant roller coaster. And they lit up the midway.

Carnival music blared everywhere. Bells rang out every time someone won a game.

"Wow! This is great!" Jeremy cried as we walked through the midway, tugging Carla behind us.

I spotted a small, dirty, white trailer in the back. A sign hung over the door. MADAME WANDA SEES ALL. HAVE YOUR FORTUNE TOLD.

"Come on!" I turned to Carla. "Let's see what Madame Wanda says about your future. Bet it isn't as scary as you think."

"No," Carla refused. "I'm too scared."

"We'll go in with you. It'll be a laugh. Bet she tells you some wild things."

Carla shook her head no.

"I'll stay out here with Carla," Harold offered. "You two can go in." Harold was scared, too.

"Harold is afraid of the future," Jeremy whispered to me, "because it's another thing he can't see!"

"We're all going in," I declared. And with that, Jeremy and I pulled Carla and Harold into Madame Wanda's trailer.

It was very dark inside, and a sweet odor filled the room. Incense, I guessed. Soft, eerie music surrounded us.

A cold green mist swirled through the air. It sent a chill down my spine. I turned to Carla. She shivered, too.

In front of us, a single candle glowed on an old table. Our shadows shifted on the walls in the flickering light.

It really was scary in here.

"H-hello," I stammered.

No answer.

I took a step forward and heard a moan.

A low moan.

My heart began to race. I glanced at the others.

Harold stood frozen in place. Jeremy looked frightened, too. In the dim light, I could see his eyes nervously dart around the room. Carla didn't move.

The moan grew louder. "Let's get out of here," I whispered.

I turned to leave. But a breeze — from nowhere — snuffed out the candle, plunging us into darkness.

We screamed.

And then we heard the voice.

"Come forward," it called from a darkened corner. We inched up. My legs trembled. The moaning grew closer. Closer.

"I — I want to go," Carla groaned. She bolted for the door, but a hand suddenly reached out and grabbed her.

Madame Wanda.

The woman struck a match and lit the candle. "Sit!" she commanded.

We sat.

She took her place at the table. She was dressed in a shiny black gown, and on her head she wore a dark-green turban.

I studied her face. Purple veins shot through the whites of her eyes. I couldn't stop staring at her eyes — and those lips. Dark, dramatic lips.

She grinned at me and her lips parted. Her dark eyes glowed, as if seeing right through me.

I jumped up, but she yanked me back down.

She stared deeply into our eyes. "Who will go first?" she asked slowly.

A trickle of sweat dripped down my forehead. I grabbed Carla's hand and raised it in the air. "She will!"

Carla snatched her hand back, but Madame Wanda reached out and seized it. Carla's hand trembled in Madame Wanda's.

"Do not be frightened," the fortune-teller said.

"I am only going to reveal your future. Nothing more."

Madame Wanda held Carla's hand tightly as she peered into her crystal ball. I glanced around the table. Jeremy and Harold sat perfectly still — statues with eyes glued to the crystal ball.

"Ahhhhh. I see something," Madame Wanda murmured. "Yes. It is becoming clearer!"

And then she gasped.

We all jumped.

Madame Wanda's face filled with horror. Her eyes bulged wide with fear. "No! No! I don't *believe* what I see in your future!" she cried.

"What? What is it?" Carla screamed. "Tell me!"

"I — I cannot. I have no choice! I cannot allow you to grow old and suffer!" Then she dropped Carla's hand — and pressed her thumb into Carla's forehead! "I have given you the Thumbprint of Doom!"

"Noooooo!" Carla shrieked. She knocked her chair over — and hurtled out of the trailer.

We all leaped up and ran after her. We found her leaning against the trailer. Gasping for breath. "The Thumbprint of Doom!" she murmured. She rubbed her forehead.

We laughed.

"Don't be afraid. It was all a joke," I explained. "We just wanted to show you how dumb superstitions are. Nothing bad will happen to you. You'll see. It was all a joke."

"Yeah," Jeremy added. "We paid Madame Wanda this morning. We paid her to say all that and press her thumb on your forehead."

"I know. I know it was a joke," Carla replied calmly. "I *knew* that woman couldn't give me the Thumbprint of Doom."

"How did you know?" I asked.

"Because only I have the power!" Carla cried. "Why do you think I believe in this stuff? Because I *know* it's all true! I know it's true — because I have the power! That's why I'm frightened of it. And now I have no choice. You know my secret. I have no choice."

Then Carla dived toward us. And before we could move, she pressed her icy thumb on our foreheads. "I've given you all the Thumbprint of Doom!" she cried.

I shrieked in horror. Carla grabbed my sleeve with an iron grip. I struggled to pull free, but she held on.

"Let me go," I cried. "Let me go!"

Carla threw back her head and laughed — a wicked laugh. She yanked on my arm. And a burning pain shot through my body.

With a burst of strength, I ripped free — and we ran.

We ran from evil Carla.

We ran from the carnival.

We ran to our doom.

* * *

Carla watched the three kids run off.

"That was a very mean joke, Carla," Madame Wanda said, stepping out of her trailer.

"They started it," Carla replied.

"How long do you think it will take them to realize that you have no powers? That you were just playing a trick on them?"

Carla giggled. "They'll figure it out after a day or so. Then maybe we'll all have a good laugh about it," she said. "I'm going to explore the carnival now. What time will you be home?"

"About ten," Madame Wanda replied.

"Okay," Carla said. "See you later, Mom."

ABOUT THE AUTHOR

R.L. STINE is the author of over three dozen best-selling thrillers and mysteries for young people. Recent titles for teenagers include *I Saw You That Night!*, *Call Waiting*, *Halloween Night II*, *The Dead Girlfriend*, and *The Baby-sitter IV*, all published by Scholastic. He is also the author of the *Fear Street* series.

Bob lives in New York City with his wife, Jane, and fifteen-year-old son, Matt.

The joke's on them!

Goosebumps®

Harry and his brother, Alex, are
dying to fit in at Camp Spirit Moon.
But this camp is so weird.
There's a goofy left-handed camp salute.
Strange blue puddles on the cabin floor.
And all of the old campers love to play jokes,
especially on new campers.
But when the jokes start to get out of hand,
Harry and Alex decide to get out of camp—
Before it's too late!

Ghost Camp

Goosebumps #45

by R.L. Stine

Appearing soon at a bookstore near you.